OSIDGE

D0545779

LONDON BOROUGH OF BARNET

30131 055065 44 2

'I'm not afraid,' she lied.

She was terrified. Thrilled. Exultant. Curious.

Lily felt her hand settle against the muscled plane of his chest. Beneath her palm beat a steady pulse that seemed leisurely compared with her own wildly careering heartbeat. He was *real*. Not the phantom lover of her dreams. He was one of the most beautiful men on the planet, and she—

She shifted back. 'This is a mistake.'

He moved with her, his thigh brushing hers. Ripples coursed up her leg to the spot between her thighs where a different pulse beat—needy and quick.

'No mistake. Admit it, Lily. This feels *right*.'

His lips touched hers again—once, twice—before settling on her mouth. For a moment he held utterly still. She absorbed the rich, warm scent of his skin, the delicious tang of him on her tongue, the long body hard up against hers and the gentleness of his hand at the back of her head, cradling, tender…

A mighty shudder ran through her—a sigh that made no s   A
sigh   e first
tim

Growing up near the beach, **Annie West** spent lots of time observing tall, burnished lifeguards—early research! Now she spends her days fantasising about gorgeous men and their love lives. Annie has been a reader all her life. She also loves travel, long walks, good company and great food. You can contact her at annie@annie-west.com or via PO Box 1041, Warners Bay, NSW 2282, Australia.

Visit the Author Profile page at
millsandboon.co.uk for more titles.

THE FLAW IN
RAFFAELE'S
REVENGE

An enormous thank you to
dear Abby Green,
who heard my plot ideas then asked
why I didn't combine them.
I loved our rare chance to talk stories!

And a huge thank you to
Franca Poli
for your support and patient assistance
with your lovely language.
Any errors are mine.

PROLOGUE

RAFFAELE PETRI POCKETED his credit card and left the waterfront restaurant. Ignoring the stares, he nodded his thanks to the waiter. The service had been excellent, attentive but not fawning, the tip well-earned.

Raffaele hadn't forgotten how it felt to depend on the goodwill of rich foreigners.

He paused, his eyes adjusting to the sunshine. The sea glittered as it slapped the whiter-than-white yachts. The salt tang was strong on the air and he breathed deep, relishing it after the overpowering perfume of the women who'd tried to catch his attention from the next table.

He sauntered past huge yachts and motor cruisers. The Marmaris waterfront was packed with ostentatious displays of wealth. Just the place to invest, if his research was right, which it always was. This trip to Turkey would be profitable and—

A bray of laughter froze his footsteps. The hoarse, distinctive sound ran up his spine like dancing skeletal fingers, pinching his skin.

Raffaele's breath rushed in like the snap of a spinnaker in a stiff breeze. The laugh came again, yanking his attention to a towering multistorey cruiser. Sunlight polished the chestnut hair of the man leaning from the upper deck, shouting encouragement at two women on the promenade.

The ground beneath Raffaele's feet seemed to heave and buckle, mirroring the tumble of his constricting gut. His hands rolled tight as he stared at the florid man waving a champagne glass at the women.

'Come on up. The bubbly's on ice.'

Raffaele knew that voice.

Even after twenty-one years he recognised it.

That smug tone, that hoarse laugh, had crept through his nightmares since he was twelve.

He'd given up hope of finding him. He'd never known the man's name and the slimy villain had disappeared from Genoa faster than a rat leaving a scuttled ship. No one had listened to a skinny twelve-year-old who'd insisted the foreigner with hair the colour of *castagne* was to blame for Gabriella's death.

Gabriella...

Fury ignited. The wrath of thwarted retribution, of loathing and grief.

The blast of emotion stunned him.

He'd spent his life perfecting the art of not feeling, not caring for anyone, not *trusting,* since Gabriella. But now... It took everything he had merely to stand still and take in the scene.

Keenly he catalogued everything, from the guy's features, grown pudgy with age and self-indulgence, to the name of the cruiser and the fact his staff, neat in white shorts and shirts, spoke English as only natives could. One of them offered to help the women aboard.

Girls, Raffaele amended, not women. Both blonde, both in their teens, though one was made up to look ten years older. Raffa was an expert on make-up and on women.

The Englishman's tastes hadn't changed. He still liked them young and blonde.

Bile rose. Raffa's heart thrashed with the need to climb aboard and deliver justice for Gabriella with his fists. There was no doubt this was the same man.

But Raffa was no longer an impulsive, grieving kid.

Now he had the power to do more than beat the man to a bloody pulp. That thought alone held him back. Even so, it was a battle to rein in his need for instant vengeance.

'Ciao, bella.' He strolled forward, curling his mouth in a half smile the camera, and millions of women the world

over, loved. Not for a second did he lift his gaze to the middle-aged man above them.

'Lucy—' The taller one nudged her companion. 'Quick. Turn around. He looks like... He couldn't be...could he?'

Two pairs of eyes widened as he approached. Twin gasps of excitement. The one who'd spoken smiled wide while her companion looked dazed.

Raffa was used to dealing with besotted fans. But instead of a nod of acknowledgement before moving on, he increased the wattage of his smile in an invitation that had never once failed.

The taller girl stepped closer, pulling her friend along, the boat and its owner forgotten. They didn't even blink as the man above them called agitated instructions for them to come aboard.

'You look just like Raffaele Petri. I suppose people say that all the time.' Her voice was breathless and young. Too young for the man on the boat. Or for Raffa. The difference was that with him she'd be safe.

'That's because I *am* Raffaele Petri.'

Twin gasps met the announcement and the smaller girl looked as if she might faint.

'Are you all right?'

She nodded, goggle-eyed, while her friend dragged out her phone. 'Do you mind?'

'Of course not.' The world was full of amateur photos of him. 'I was going to get a coffee.' He gestured to a street leading away from the waterfront. 'Care to join me?'

The girls were so busy chattering as they walked that only Raffa heard the Englishman's abusive yells. He'd been deprived of his afternoon's amusement.

Soon he'd be deprived of everything that mattered to him.

The Englishman wouldn't escape again. Justice would be sweet.

This time Raffa's smile was genuine.

CHAPTER ONE

'STOP PULLING MY LEG, Pete.' Lily leaned back from the desk and shifted her grip on the phone. 'It's been a long day. You might be just waking up in New York but it's bedtime in Australia.'

Looking towards the window, she saw the reflection of her office in the glass. Her house was too far from town for street lights and the stars wouldn't show till she switched off her lamp. She rubbed her stiff neck. Completing this project within deadline and to her own exacting standards had been tough.

'No joke.' Pete's usually laid-back voice with its Canadian accent sounded excited. 'The boss wants you here and he never jokes about business.'

Lily straightened in her seat, her pulse thudding. 'You're serious?'

'Absolutely. And what the boss wants, the boss makes a policy of getting. You know that.'

'Except Raffaele Petri isn't my boss.' Even saying his name aloud seemed somehow ridiculous. What could she, ordinary Lily Nolan, living in a rundown farmhouse an hour south of Sydney, have in common with Raffaele Petri? 'He doesn't know I exist.'

Petri inhabited a stellar plane ordinary mortals only dreamed of or read about in gossip magazines, while she...

Lily dropped the hand she'd lifted to her cheek. She hated that old, nervous gesture.

'Of course he knows. Why do you think you've had so much work from us? He was impressed with your report for the Tahiti deal and asked for you on every one since.'

Lily blinked. She'd never imagined Signor Petri himself

reading her research reports. She'd assumed he had other things to do with his time, like indulging himself at the world's most luxurious fleshpots.

'That's fantastic, Pete. I can't tell you how pleased I am.' Despite her recent success, the size of the loan she'd taken to buy this house and expand the business kept her awake at night. But after years feeling like an outsider she'd been driven by the need to establish her own place in the world, something *she'd* achieved and could be proud of. Even though it meant moving across the continent from her anxious family. She needed this to turn her life around.

Tight muscles eased. If Signor Petri had personally commented on her work—

'Excellent. You'll find the contract in your inbox. It will be great finally putting a face to the voice once you're working here.'

'Whoa. Wait a minute.' Lily shot to her feet. 'I meant I'm pleased to have what I do valued. That's all.' She drove herself to excel and knew her service was first class, but it was reassuring having it confirmed by her most influential customer, especially now she had this mortgage.

'You *don't* want to accept the boss's offer to work here?' Pete's hushed tone made it sound as if she'd refused mankind's only chance to find a cure for cancer.

'That's right.' The thought of being in a city, surrounded by millions of people, being *seen* by strangers every day, made her flesh crawl as if she were breaking into hives. She even avoided driving into her small town when possible, opting to have her groceries delivered. Working in New York, constantly facing curious stares, would be a nightmare. It was one thing to be confident about your work and your worth, quite another to run the gauntlet of constant public interest.

'You're joking. Who wouldn't want to work for Raffaele Petri?'

Lily threaded her fingers through her long hair, pushing

it from her face. 'I already work for him, off and on.' Her contract work for his company had been so lucrative it had made her enormous mortgage possible. The prestige of his name on those regular contracts had convinced even the cautious loans officer. 'But I'm my own boss. Why would I want to change that?'

Her independence, her ability to *control* her life, meant everything. Perhaps because her world had been impacted irrevocably by a single, senseless event that had robbed her of so much.

A moment's silence told her how bizarre her attitude seemed.

'Let's see. The kudos for a start. Work for him and you can walk into any job you like. He only employs the best. Then there's the salary. Read the contract before you reject it, Lily. Chances like this don't just come along.'

His tone was urgent. But Lily knew what was right for her.

'Thanks for your interest, Pete. I appreciate it, really I do. But it's not possible.' She forked her hand through her hair again, for a millisecond wondering what opportunities she might have pursued if her life had been different. If *she* were different.

She dropped her hand, disgusted with herself. She couldn't change the past. Everything she wanted, everything she aspired to, was within her grasp. All she had to do was work towards her goals. Success, security, self-sufficiency. *That* was what she wanted. Not jostling with commuters or being a drone in a corporation. Or hankering after places she'd never visit.

'Lily, you can't have considered. At least think about it.'

'I have, Pete, but the answer is no. I'm happy here.'

At first she thought the chirruping noise was the dawn chorus. Each morning magpies and cockatoos greeted the first light. But this was too monotone, too persistent. Groaning, Lily opened her eyes. It was still night.

Pulse thundering, she groped for the phone. No one rang at this time unless it was an emergency.

'Hello?' She struggled to sit up, shoving her pillow behind her back.

'Ms Lily Nolan?'

The pulse that an instant ago had sprinted in her arteries gave a single mighty thump. The deep male voice was foreign, rich and dark like a shot of espresso.

She groped for the bedside light and squinted at her watch. Minutes to midnight. No wonder she felt groggy. She'd only slept half an hour.

'Who's speaking?'

'Raffaele Petri.'

Raffaele Petri!

To her sleep-addled senses that voice sounded like liquid seduction. She frowned and pulled the neck of her sleep shirt closed. Male voices didn't affect her that way. But then how many sounded like this?

'Are you still there?'

'Of course I'm here. I've just woken up.'

'*Mi dispiace.*' *I'm sorry.*

He didn't sound sorry. He sounded...

Lily shook her head. If it *was* Raffaele Petri this was business. She couldn't afford to think about how potently male he sounded. Even if her hormones were dancing at the sound of that deliciously accented voice.

'Signor Petri—' She raked her hair from her face, shuffling higher in the bed. 'What can I do for you?'

'Sign the contract and get here *subito*.'

Lily choked down her instinctive response. The only place she was going *subito*, immediately, was back to sleep.

'That's impossible.'

'Nonsense. It's the only sensible course of action.'

Lily breathed deep, letting the chilly night air fill her

lungs as she sought calm. He wasn't only her client, he was her most important client.

'Did you hear me?'

'Yes.'

'Good. When you've arranged your flight give my assistant the details. He'll organise for you to be met at the airport.'

This must be how Renaissance Italian princes had sounded. As if every word they spoke was law. Imagine having such confidence you'd always get what you desired.

'Thank you, but I won't be contacting Pete.' She cleared her throat, her voice still husky from sleep. 'I was very flattered by your offer, Signor Petri, but I prefer working for myself.'

'You're turning me down?' His soft voice raised the hairs on the back of her neck.

Had anyone ever denied Raffaele Petri what he wanted?

Lily's heart thudded. She was on dangerous ground.

Widely touted as the most beautiful man in the world, he'd become famous as the golden-haired, outrageously handsome face, and body, that had turned designer casual into a style men around the globe aspired to emulate. No doubt he'd had women saying yes all his life.

But he had far more than looks. After leaving modelling he'd defied the critics and proven himself über-successful in business. Wealthy and powerful, Raffaele Petri was clearly used to instant compliance.

'I'm very flattered by the offer—'

'But?' That purr of enquiry barely concealed a razor-sharp edge.

Lily drew in a slow breath. 'Unfortunately I'm not in a position to accept.'

Silence. Long enough for her to wonder if she'd burned her bridges. Fear skated through her. She needed the work his company sent.

'What would have to change so you'd be in a position to accept?'

Damn the man. Why couldn't he just accept no?

'May I ask instead why you want me?' For a nanosecond heat surged at the unintentional double meaning of her words. But the idea of Raffaele Petri wanting her for anything other than work was so utterly unbelievable it rapidly faded. 'I was told you were happy with my research and our current arrangement.'

'If I were unhappy with your work I wouldn't offer you a job, Ms Nolan.' His clipped tones twisted her tension higher. 'I want you here on my team because you're the best at what you do. Simple as that.'

The heat suffusing her this time came from gratification. 'Thank you, Signor Petri. I appreciate your good opinion.' She'd love to ask about a testimonial but the throbbing silence told her this wasn't the time. 'Please know I'll continue to offer the best possible service.' She wriggled back against the pillow.

'That's not enough.'

'Sorry?' What more could he want than her best?

'I'm starting a significant project.' He paused. 'I need my team on hand and bound by the utmost confidentiality.'

Lily stiffened. 'I hope you're not implying I'm a security risk. Every contract I accept is completed in strictest confidence. I safeguard my research and my clients.' She never shared details of clients without permission. Which was why it would have been a coup to have a testimonial from him on her website.

She'd begun as a researcher for a private enquiry firm but the cases got her down. She'd found her niche when she widened her horizons—from staff checks to analyses of businesses and commercial trends. Lately it had been the viability of new ventures or businesses ripe for takeover.

That was where Raffaele Petri came in. The man was like a shark scenting blood before his competitors. Every time she investigated a business for him she'd discovered vulnerabilities and problems. It was the magic of the man that, once he acquired them, he turned those businesses into some of the most successful in the leisure industry, from a glamorous resort in Tahiti to a marina and yacht-building company in Turkey.

'If I doubted your ability to keep a secret I wouldn't hire you.'

Lily released a breath, relief rising.

'But,' he added, 'I can't afford risks. This team will be the best of the best. And it will be in New York. I need you here.'

Pride swelled. Lily had never been *needed*. Never stood out. Looks, school grades, sport, she'd always been average, never in the limelight until—

Lily shook her head in self-disgust at that old neediness. It was a spill over from her teenage years when she'd felt no one really wanted her, that to her family she was only a burden and a worry. And to her friends an embarrassing, constant reminder of a disaster they'd rather forget. She'd hated that awareness of being included out of duty rather than because her peers wanted her around.

His words made her long to say, *Yes, of course, I'll be in New York tomorrow.*

Imagine exploring the Big Apple. Imagine…

She swallowed hard. It wasn't possible. Facing the curious eyes of all those strangers, seeing them stare in fascination or hurriedly turn away. She wouldn't put herself through that anymore.

'I'm used to working with your staff from a distance. I'm sure—'

'That's not the way this project will proceed, Ms Nolan.' His words were staccato, tiny darts pricking her skin. 'I won't tolerate failure on this one.'

Lily opened her mouth to say that if his project failed it wouldn't be down to her.

'Yes, Ms Nolan? You were saying?'

'I'm sorry I can't accommodate you, Signor Petri.'

'I'll double the salary. And the bonus on completion.'

Lily's eyes widened. She'd been curious enough to check the contract and the salary had staggered her. It was more than she'd earn in two years. The thought of four years' income in one hit was so tempting. It would solve her financial worries...

'Changing your tune, Ms Nolan? I thought you might.' That voice was smug now, making her want to hiss her displeasure. At him for thinking she could be bought? Or at herself for being tempted despite knowing it couldn't happen?

Part of her still hankered after adventure, travel, excitement. But she'd had to push those dreams aside when her life had derailed at fourteen. She'd been robbed of her best friend, her carefree youth, her 'normal' life. She'd even missed out on things everyone else took for granted like flirting with boys and dating.

She shook her head, long tresses slipping over her cheeks. Curse the man for stirring longings she'd put behind her years before.

She loved her home, was proud she'd saved enough to be buying it. But it was more than that. Lily *needed* the security and peace it provided. The sense of refuge.

'No, Signor Petri. That was the sound of surprise but not agreement.'

'Interesting, Ms Nolan. Most people would jump at this opportunity. Why aren't you? A family, is that it? You have a husband and children perhaps?'

'No! I don't—' Lily clamped her lips shut before she blurted out anything else. Instinctively she felt safer keeping her private life private from this man.

'No family? I thought you sounded a little young for one.'

Lily's eyebrows arched. At twenty-eight she wasn't so young. Or was he implying she didn't sound professional?

Or maybe he's just winding you up. This man enjoyed playing with her, like a cat with a trapped mouse.

Like a bully wielding his superior power.

Lily's chin shot up. 'I suppose age becomes important when one reaches…*mature* years.'

A little huff of sound reached her over the long distance. A gasp of irritation or, could it be, stifled laughter?

She shouldn't have said it. The veiled reference to his age, five years her senior, was indiscreet and possibly ruinous. But she refused to sit like a pincushion to be needled.

'Fortunately I'm not quite in my dotage, Ms Nolan.'

No, he wasn't. She kept seeing photos of him at glamorous functions. Always with a sophisticated woman on his arm, but never the same one.

'So if you don't have a family to tie you there it must be a lover.' His voice dipped low, like dark treacle rolling through her veins to eddy in her belly. Lily drew her knees up, pressing them to her chest, trying to kill the unsettling sensation.

'My private life is no concern of yours, Signor Petri.' Did he hear the wobble of fury in her voice?

'But it is, Ms Nolan, when it comes between me and what I want.'

'Then it's time you discovered you can't always get what you want.' The words poured out. 'I decide when and where I sell my services.'

Lily scrubbed a shaky hand over her face, her chest heaving. This was going from bad to worse. Anger and anxiety curdled her insides. And self-disgust. She needed to stay calm, no matter what the provocation.

'I assume you don't normally speak to your clients in that suggestively sexy voice.' His own voice was far too sultry. 'It would give them the wrong idea about what services you sell.'

Lily almost dropped the phone.

Suggestively sexy?

He had to be kidding! No man had ever called her sexy.

Of course he's kidding. He's playing with you, searching for your weak spots.

And finding them!

Curiously, the realisation calmed her, despite the burn of annoyance.

'There are reasons I can't work for you in New York, Signor Petri, but—'

'Name three.'

'Sorry?'

'I want to know why you reject my offer. Come on, three sound reasons.' The words shot out, quick and demanding, and before she knew it, Lily was answering.

'I don't have a passport for a start.' She winced. That made her sound like some country hick to a man who travelled the world as easily as she travelled it vicariously via the internet.

'That's one. What else?'

'I can't afford to rent a place in New York.'

'Not even with the bonus I'm offering?'

'I have commitments here. Any money I earn goes to those.'

'And the third? What's your third reason?'

Because she couldn't stand the thought of working in an office with other people? Because she wouldn't put herself through all that again?

Because she preferred solitude? She had a good life and an exciting business plan and no bullying magnate was going to disrupt those on a whim.

'You don't answer, Ms Nolan, which makes me think it's the most important reason of all. Or you don't have one.'

Sheer strength of will stopped Lily from blurting a response. He wasn't going to goad her again.

'Is it a lover holding you back?'

'You have no right to quiz me like this.'

'I have every right when it stymies my most important deal.'

Despite his monumental arrogance, Lily's ears pricked up. She was fascinated by this man's business acumen, his ability to see opportunities before anyone else. She'd love to know what this secret project was.

'You want my advice?' She was in the process of saying 'No' when he spoke over top of her. 'Ditch him, Ms Nolan. Find yourself a man who won't obstruct such a brilliant opportunity. You've got real talent. You shouldn't let him stand in the way of it.'

For a second Lily gawped. Raffaele Petri was beyond belief. If she had a partner she'd never leave him on the say-so of some self-important stranger.

'I wasn't aware you were an expert on relationships, Signor Petri. Aren't your girlfriends famous for being short-term?'

Lily gasped as she heard her thoughts slip out. She'd just scuttled her future with his company. But his behaviour, his whole attitude, was offensive.

A crack of laughter sounded on the line, resolving into a warm chuckle that did strange things to her insides.

Lily stiffened as fire tongued her sensitive flesh. A hot shiver ripped through her as if a warm masculine hand, rather than a disembodied voice, caressed her. She swallowed hard, horrified at her instantaneous response.

Wasn't it enough that the man looked like a Greek god come to life? Did he have to sound irresistible too? Lily pressed the heel of her palm to her sternum, trying to ease her heart's wild pounding.

She detested bullies. Her response was inexplicable.

Except it wasn't. She was a young, healthy woman, with the physical urges that went with that. Her hormones didn't care if he was a saint or the devil incarnate. All they cared about was that they'd been deprived of anything like excitement or satisfaction for far too long.

'Don't laugh at me!' Her words rapped out, too short, too sharp.

In the sudden silence she realised what she'd revealed. He knew he'd got to her.

Raffaele Petri might be a bully but he was clever. All the world knew he came from the backstreets of some large Italian city. His business success was a commercial miracle.

'What if I'm laughing at myself? Finally being called on my defects.' His voice held an edge but she couldn't tell if it was amusement or banked fury. 'My decrepit age. My lack of emotional staying power. What else, I wonder?' He paused. 'Have you been investigating me, Ms Nolan?'

Despite the rich cadence of his voice, Lily heard the threat in that low purr of sound.

'I haven't, Signor Petri. Your business, yes, before I agreed to work for it. But as for a personal profile...' She shook her head, her hair swirling. 'That wasn't necessary.'

'Because the paparazzi do such a thorough job of portraying someone's life, don't they?'

Lily frowned. Was that emotion? Had she hit a nerve?

'The passport can be fast-tracked. I'll get my people onto it. Accommodation will be arranged. Plus I'll have the contract altered to include the increased salary and bonus.' He paused, which was as well, because her head was spinning. His abrupt change of subject left her floundering. 'Appealing enough for you?'

The silence that followed was thick with expectation. He was waiting for her to agree before he hung up and dealt with whatever issue was next on his list.

Except Lily wasn't some problem to be fixed.

'I appreciate the offer, the very handsome offer,' she choked out, her fingers clamping the phone. 'But it won't work for me. I'm happy to do whatever I can from here—'

'But that won't work for *me*.' His voice sent a trickle of foreboding down her backbone.

For ten seconds there was silence. For twenty. But Lily

refused to back down. What he asked was impossible for her and she had too much pride to explain why.

'You leave me no choice, Ms Nolan. We'll find some-one else to be principal researcher.'

Lily eased back against her pillow, shaky as the tension gripping her body finally began to abate.

'And my company won't hire you again.'

Lily couldn't stifle a hiss of shock. Air locked some-where between her throat and her lungs as her body froze. Stars scattered her vision, dimming to pinpricks till, with a sagging release, her lungs began pumping again.

Without his business, hers was dead in the water. Four months ago she'd have weathered the setback but not now. Not since the loan and the expansion.

If she couldn't meet the repayments she'd lose every-thing—her work and her home. The life she'd so pains-takingly built.

'Did you say something, Ms Nolan?'

Lily gulped to clear her throat but couldn't think of a thing to say.

'It won't take long for my dissatisfaction with your ser-vice to get out, either. You'd be surprised how fast news spreads. Continental boundaries don't mean anything and I have contacts around the world. From Melbourne to Mum-bai, London to Los Angeles.'

Again that lethal pause, allowing her time to process the bleak scenario he'd painted. Her name would be mud with the really big enterprises, the internationals she'd set her sights on to make her expanded business a success.

'You'll go out of your way to blacken my name?' Her voice was a thin scratch of sound but at least it was steady. Unlike the rest of her. She shook as if with fever.

'I'll be sure to mention it whenever appropriate.' In other words he'd take delight in savaging her reputation.

Hatred coiled, tightening in her belly. Hatred as she'd only ever felt once before, for the guy who'd changed her life in an instant—from carefree to a grim round of medical treatments. Her hand lifted to her face.

Swallowing hard, Lily turned the nervous gesture into a defiant flick of the wrist, sending her long hair flying back from her face. Deliberately she set her chin, staring at her face reflected in the window.

One thing Raffaele Petri didn't know—she was a fighter. She'd survived far worse than he could dish out and emerged stronger as a result.

She lowered her hand, smoothing the quilt as she dragged in aching breaths. She opened her mouth to speak but he beat her to it.

'Of course if you were to change your mind...'

Fury swamped her. He knew she had no choice.

Even so, part of her brain noted that the snake in the Garden of Eden must have sounded like this. No hissing, no sharpness. Just a lush, seductive roll of sound that invited her to go against everything she knew and trusted. To take the plunge, even though it must end in disaster.

'You're nothing if not predictable, Signor Petri.' She pressed the phone to her ear but heard no response. 'Textbook bullying, in fact.'

Still nothing. His silence infuriated her but she refused to give him the satisfaction of hearing her rant. She looked at her hand, fisted so tight in her lap it was hard to prise open. When she did she saw scarlet crescents where her nails had scored.

'Very well, Signor Petri. I'll work for you.' Her lungs ached as she released the breath crammed in her chest. 'But you can change the contract to three times the original salary. Ditto with the bonus. Have it in my inbox tomorrow and if it's satisfactory I'll sign.' She paused, trying to control her sharp, shallow breaths.

To her astonishment he didn't disagree.

'I'll see you in New York, Ms Nolan.'

Not if I see you first.

She might be stuck working for him but she had no illusions he'd be part of the project team. He'd be sunning himself in the Bahamas or skiing in Switzerland or whatever the wealthy did when they weren't harassing ordinary people. Somehow she'd deal with the travel and all those people. She'd do the job, take his money and come back to build her future here as she'd planned.

She'd get through this.

'Goodbye, Signor Petri.'

'Not goodbye. *Arrivederci*, Ms Nolan.'

CHAPTER TWO

RAFFA GOT TO the office after a breakfast meeting.

Across the large room he saw an unfamiliar figure—
long hair, loose shirt, loose trousers and flat shoes. The
clothes were resolutely unfeminine but the body beneath
all that unflattering drabness wasn't. Femininity was there
in the way she moved, despite her rigid back and high
shoulders.

It had to be Lily Nolan. The area was off-limits to all
but his hand-picked team.

She'd been tense on the phone that night too. Uptight
and angry, yet that husky, just-awake voice had done things
to him no woman had in years.

He frowned at the unwanted memory.

Raffa's eyes narrowed on the rhythmic swish of hair
down her narrow back as she walked away. It all but
reached her waist. Not blonde or black or even dark but
simply brown. A brown so ordinary and unremarkable it
looked uncompromising, as if she spurned most women's
desire to improve on nature with eye-catching colour.

He turned into his private office and took a seat, gesturing for his assistant to do the same. Through the glass
walls he saw Lily Nolan talking with someone by the door
to the conference room. Her body language radiated stress,
right down to the fist clenching at her side.

Had he made a mistake bringing her here? He'd wanted
her because of her talents, her often brilliant insights and
her professionalism. He knew she'd go the extra mile to
meet his needs.

But that night on the phone her obstinacy, the way she
challenged him as no one else dared, had piqued his inter-

est. He'd accepted her outrageous terms because every re-
fusal she gave made him more determined to win.

The knowledge he'd acted on a whim had annoyed him
ever since. He never allowed himself to be sidetracked.
He'd got where he was by grabbing every opportunity to
build his wealth and success. Even if some of those opportunities were unpalatable, they'd been necessary. He was
never impulsive.

'How's our newest staff member fitting in? Any problems?'

'No, nothing like that.'

Was that a flush on Pete's boyish face? Raffa felt his eyebrows cinch together. The woman had been here less than
a day. Surely she hadn't seduced his PA already?

'She's hit the ground running. She must be jet-lagged
but she's already got acquainted with our set up here. Now
she's meeting the rest of the team.' Pete swivelled his head
towards the conference room, his gaze fixed.

Raffa realised it wasn't adoration on his assistant's face
but something he couldn't read.

'Yet she makes you uncomfortable?'

Pete's face mottled red. Embarrassment? Lust?

'Of course not.' The words tumbled out too quickly.
'She's very professional.'

Professional. It sounded like faint praise. Especially
since in the past he'd overheard Pete laughing with the
woman over a long-distance connection.

'But?' Raffa fixed him with a stern gaze. His policy was
to remove problems the instant they arose. If this woman
disrupted the smoothly oiled workings of his team he'd
take action immediately.

Pete shrugged. 'You know how it is when you know
someone only from a distance. You build up a picture in
your mind. The reality can be...different.' He gestured
abruptly to the tablet he carried. 'About the review of the

Hawaiian hotel. Will I bring that forward? You'd mentioned a snap inspection to keep them on their toes.'

Raffa surveyed his PA, reading his discomfort. It was probably as Pete said—the deflating reality of the first face-to-face meeting. But Raffa never left anything to chance.

He'd planned to leave the rebellious Australian alone today to get on with the job for which he was paying such an exorbitant salary. And he would   after he'd checked her out.

'We're busy wrapping up some other projects but anything you need on the legal side, let me know.' Consuela Flores gave a brisk nod and smile from the end of the conference table and Lily felt herself sink back in her seat, a grateful answering smile on her face.

Among the group she'd be working with, the middle-aged lawyer had proved the easiest to deal with. Her severe demeanour, magenta power suit, expensive pearls and stiffly lacquered hair had made Lily wary. Here was an imposing woman for whom appearance as well as performance was important. Yet after a millisecond of silence when they met and that brief, predictable widening of the eyes, Ms Flores had treated Lily like everyone else around the table.

Lily had wanted to hug her for that.

This morning had been tough, every bit as difficult as she'd feared. Her hands were clammy, her chest weighted and her pulse still too fast. Forcing herself into the office had been a major test of nerves already strung out from the stress of travelling.

'Thanks, I appreciate that. For now, though, I suspect it won't be legal expertise I need. There'll be a lot of digging first.'

Consuela nodded. 'I'm glad it's you doing the digging. Your reports for the Turkish deal made our work much easier. There's nothing like heading into negotiations well-prepared, with no lurking pitfalls. Now you're onsite we can touch base as anything arises.'

Lily's smile grew, the clamp on her chest easing a little.

Only the knowledge she was up to this job, more than up to it, had got her across the Pacific, across the United States and into this building, when all she wanted was to lock herself inside her home and not budge.

She could do this, no matter how horribly far out of her comfort zone she felt.

No, she wouldn't just do the job. She'd excel! Her work meant everything. It was the one part of her world where she had complete control, complete confidence.

Which made it all the more infuriating that she'd been nauseous with nerves today. Fronting up at the office was the most difficult thing she'd done in years.

See what happens when you lock yourself away all the time?

Now it's you with the problem, not them.

Lily banished the voice in her head. She didn't have time for self-doubt.

'I'm looking forward to working with you too, Consuela.'

She darted a glance around the table. The woman from finance in retro-trendy glasses quickly turned her head as if she'd been watching the lawyer, not Lily. But she was too slow. Besides, the distressed twist of her lips, as if she felt ill, betrayed her.

Further down the table the guy from acquisitions flushed as Lily turned to him. Like Pete, Raffaele Petri's PA, he found looking at her embarrassing. Beside him the older man from systems management didn't even try, instead staring past her shoulder.

Lily sat straighter, determined not to be daunted.

Yet that didn't stop the sick feeling in her stomach, or the churning memories of her previous forays into office work. Each one a disaster. Eventually she'd given up trying and decided to work from the seclusion of home.

The fingers of her right hand twitched but she repressed the urge to raise her hand to her face. It had taken years to cure herself of the habit and she wasn't starting again now. No matter how exposed she felt before these strangers.

'I appreciate you all making time to meet me on my first day. I'll look forward to working with you.'

Liar!

'I have a question, though.' Lily looked to Consuela. 'We all have different areas of responsibility, but is there a team leader? Without coordination we'll have problems.'

'That would be me.' The masculine voice curled around her like warm smoke.

Her heart jolted and a prickling spread across her skin.

She'd only heard that voice once but its echo had lurked in her subconscious since, visiting in those moments between waking and sleep when she was most vulnerable.

Was that heat flushing her cheeks?

It couldn't be. She'd spent half her life being gawked at. She'd lost the ability to blush in her teens.

Reluctantly she turned her head.

It was a good thing she was sitting.

Raffaele Petri's face was known around the globe. Yet the photos hadn't prepared her. Tall, taller than she'd expected with his Italian heritage. Wide shoulders, slim hips, long legs—the epitome of masculinity in its prime. Oddly his casual jacket and open-necked shirt emphasised rather than detracted from the power she sensed in him. He didn't need a three-piece suit to stamp his authority.

Chiselled features that looked too close to perfection to be true. She'd assumed those photos had been airbrushed. Yes, there were crinkles around his eyes, as if from time in the sun, but perversely that only made him more attractive. Hair the colour of dark old gold, tidy but hinting at tousled. Enough to make her fingers twitch at the thought

of touching. The hooded cast of his eyes looked languor-
ous until you met that piercing blue stare.

Lily swallowed over a ball of sandpaper in her throat.
Meeting his gaze was a palpable experience, as if he'd
reached out and taken her hand. Sizzling heat ran through
her as those eyes held hers—compelling, electric.

It wasn't just that he was ridiculously handsome, she
realised as she forced a slow breath out. He was...*more*.
Even from the other side of the conference table she felt
the crackle of energy, the sense he was a man who made
things happen.

Unhurriedly he surveyed her, cataloguing everything
from the hair brushing her cheeks to her face, her throat
and down as far as was visible above the table.

The old resentment rose, that he should scrutinise her
like some animal in a cage. Till she realised she'd done the
same—taking in his appearance in minute detail.

The knowledge sapped her anger, leaving her winded
as his gaze lifted.

'At last we meet, Ms Nolan.'

So that explained it.

Realisation slammed into Raffa like a fist to the chest, so
strong it felt like recognition. An unexpected hit of adrenaline.

But recognition implied a link with the woman on the
far side of the table. That was nonsense, even if the memory of her husky voice and feisty attitude had intruded at
the oddest times these past weeks. The pulse of energy he
felt could only be satisfaction at getting to the bottom of
his PA's discomfort.

Lily Nolan's long hair framed an oval face that should
have been, at best, ordinary. Brown eyes, a mouth neither
thin-lipped nor lush, an unremarkable nose. Beautiful she
wasn't, but she might have been pretty if it weren't for the

wide swathe of tight, shiny skin that ran from her temple down one cheek to her jaw.

Scars faded with time. How long had she had this? The colour wasn't livid and she'd had plastic surgery. It must have been a hell of a sight before that.

Not a knife wound. He'd seen enough in his youth to realise no knife marked like this.

A burn? Some other trauma?

'Signor Petri.' That familiar voice stirred something unaccustomed that for a heartbeat distracted him.

He circled the table, arm extended.

She hesitated then pushed her chair back to stand. Her long, buttoned-up shirt fell loose around her slim frame. Again her choice of clothes hit him. A deliberate attempt not to fit in? To make the point she was here under sufferance? As if he cared what his staff wore so long as they did their work.

Her hand clasped his. Smooth and cool and small.

She just topped his shoulder in her flat shoes, tilting her head to meet his eyes. At the movement her hair slid back off her cheek, revealing more of that shiny, scarred flesh. But it wasn't the blemish that drew his attention, it was the bright challenge in her eyes.

'I believe this is where I'm supposed to say it's a pleasure to meet you, Signor Petri.'

A gasp from the other side of the room reminded him of the staff still there.

Raffa held her hand in an easy grasp, not ready to let go.

'That's right,' he murmured, bestowing a small smile. He'd won their little contest of wills and could afford to be gracious.

Yet he saw no softening in that stern expression, no easing in her rigidity. Not even a hint of response in those serious eyes.

Surprise flickered. It was rare to find someone genuinely unresponsive to his charm.

Lily Nolan grew more interesting by the moment.

'It's definitely a pleasure to meet you, Lily.' He widened his smile just a fraction, lingering on her name. 'I've been looking forward to having you here as part of the team.'

Silence for just a moment too long. 'So I gather, since you went to such lengths to get me here.'

Another muffled sound came from nearby but Raffa didn't turn. He didn't care what anyone thought.

'You were certainly elusive.'

He waited, expecting her to pull her hand from his. Instead she stood, unmoving but for the fine vibration coursing from her hand to his. She was wound up tight, bottling in strong emotion.

Yet her eyes met his directly, nothing but challenge to be read there.

This woman would make a hell of a poker player. She betrayed no hint of weakness or discomfort.

His gaze zeroed in on a minuscule movement at the corner of her mouth. For a moment he wondered if it could be the scar pulling at her mouth, till he remembered there'd been no distortion of her lips when she spoke. The tiny flicker of movement was what then? Her biting her cheek?

'Did you want me for something now?' She looked pointedly at their joined hands and Raffa felt amusement bubble. She was so patently determined to be unimpressed. So ostentatiously unaffected by his looks or position. Perversely he liked it.

How long since he'd done anything, gone anywhere, and been treated like an average Joe?

It was a novelty he hadn't known he craved till a slip of a woman with muddy brown eyes looked at him as if he wasn't anything special.

'As a matter of fact, now is the perfect time to brief you in more detail about my expectations.' He turned and nodded to Pete. Moments later his stalwart PA had emptied the room and closed the door on them.

If Lily Nolan was intimidated she didn't show it. Her hand lay unresisting in his, as if making the point his touch was immaterial to her.

Who was this woman? She'd intrigued him from their first contact.

Raffa's world and the people in it were predictable. Mostly they wanted something from him—reflected fame, an 'in' to the best circles, business opportunities, sex. Everyone wanted something.

Except this woman who didn't want him at all.

Was that why she fascinated him? Because he'd grown bored?

Raffa released his hold. He had more significant things to concentrate on than the novelty of an employee who resented his authority.

Yet he admired the way she slowly slid her hand away, not snatching it, though he'd touched her far too long. Nor did she move back, but stood, taking stock as he did.

His eyes dipped to her loose, unattractive clothing. She'd gone too far with the dressing down, the not being just another cog in his corporate wheel.

Unless she dressed that way because the scar on her face wasn't the only one. Did she have other injuries that made it uncomfortable to wear fitted clothes? The thought stirred discomfort.

Because he'd brought her here against her wishes? The idea was ludicrous. Whatever her problems, he wasn't responsible for them. He employed her at an outrageously high salary and hitherto unheard of bonuses.

'Take a seat.' He gestured to the chair she'd vacated and sank into one beside it. He was determined to understand this woman. Then he could push her from his thoughts and get on with business.

She sat watching him, feet flat on the floor, hands clasped loosely. For all the world as if he, not she, was the one whose work had to impress.

Raffa felt his lips twitch. If ever he needed another negotiator on his acquisitions team he could do far worse than Lily Nolan.

Lily read that quirk of his sculpted lips and knew she amused him.

An icicle of frozen rage jabbed her side. She wanted to cry out but kept her mouth closed and her face calm. She'd weathered enough pity, horror, revulsion and sympathy to last a lifetime. A self-important tycoon who laughed at her because she wasn't a perfectly tailored, respectful employee hardly mattered.

Or was he amused by how unfeminine she looked? His inspection had raked her from head to toe.

Remarkably, though he'd surveyed her damaged face his gaze hadn't lingered longer there than anywhere else. Almost as if her scar were no more significant than the shape of her nose or the comfy shoes she'd grabbed rather than teeter in the unaccustomed heels she'd bought in a moment of weakness. As if a pair of shoes would transform her into just another office worker!

Not with her face.

Was that what amused him? The difference between his bronzed beauty and her marred features?

She swallowed hard, tasting sharp bitterness. She was jumping to conclusions. Raffaele Petri was selfish and ruthless. She had no proof he was shallow and cruel.

But the day was young.

It wouldn't be the first time someone had used her as a foil for their own beauty. In her final year at school a couple of new girls had befriended her, both beautiful, blonde and bubbly. For the first time in years Lily had felt accepted and valued. Till she overheard them discussing how letting her hang out with them made people see them as sympathetic and even prettier than they were.

Lily shoved the memories away, drawing back her shoulders, imagining strength streaming through her spine and lifted chin. Whatever his game, she was his match. She might not be much to look at but she'd developed a strength of purpose few could equal.

Silence stretched but she refused to fill it. If this was a test of willpower he'd be disappointed.

Eyes the colour of the Pacific Ocean met hers, piercing as if reading her thoughts.

'You're settled into your office?'

She nodded. 'Yes, thank you. Pete showed me around.'

To her horror she'd discovered the floor full, not of little rabbit-hutch cubicles where workers could hide from public view, but of spacious glassed-in offices that reduced noise levels but left everyone on show.

Worse was the fact her office was beside Pete and Raffaele Petri. The idea of working with this man watching her made something shrivel inside.

'And your accommodation? It's comfortable?'

Lily nodded. The size and luxury had overwhelmed her, reminding her she was a country girl, out of her depth in sophisticated New York. Fortunately jet lag had got the better of her last night before she'd had a chance to explore properly and feel like too much of a misfit. This morning she'd overslept and had to rush to get ready. All she'd really seen was the sybaritic black marble bathroom and the inside of her suitcase as she hunted for clothes.

'Yes, thank you. It's quite sufficient.'

'Sufficient?' His mouth kicked up in a smile that did strange things to her pulse, turning it from steady to riotous. It was bad enough when he'd smiled before. He'd looked so compellingly handsome he'd stolen her breath. But this was different—genuine, and more powerful for it.

'What's so amusing?' She sat straighter.

His eyes zeroed in on hers and a fizzle of heat zapped her bones. 'I've never heard my penthouse described as merely *sufficient*.'

CHAPTER THREE

'Your penthouse?' Lily couldn't hide the shock in her voice. 'I'm staying in your *penthouse*?' Her fingers dug at her chair's leather arms.

'No other floor has a roof garden or swimming pool.' He surveyed her as if analysing a curious specimen.

For the second time that day she felt almost like she were blushing.

'I didn't open the blinds. It was late and I was jet-lagged and—' She snapped her mouth shut before she blurted out any more. She'd had a vague impression of a spacious sitting room, of stylish furnishings, but she'd never dreamed...

'Never mind, you'll see the roof garden later.'

Lily shook her head. 'There won't be a later. I can't stay there.'

'But you said the accommodation was perfectly adequate.' This time his mouth didn't curl in a smile but she knew he was laughing at her. How could he not be when she was too thick to realise she'd spent the night in a Manhattan penthouse?

'It's your home. It wouldn't be appropriate.'

Raffa couldn't imagine any of the women he'd dated turning down an opportunity to move into his apartment, even if just the guest quarters. They'd see it as a stepping stone to more.

He'd known Lily Nolan was different from the moment she picked up the phone and spoke in that sultry midnight voice. It had evoked a fragile tendril of something—not quite arousal, but definite interest.

She continued to pique his interest. She was…refreshing. Intriguing. Not because of her damaged face or appalling clothes. He, of all people, was the last person to judge on looks.

How many years since he'd found any woman interesting?

He leaned closer, registering her subtle shift as she compensated by pressing back into her chair.

Did she dislike men or just him?

The fact he wondered pulled him up short.

He wouldn't be distracted into musing on Lily Nolan's likes and dislikes. But he *did* need to ensure he'd made the right decision, bringing her here. Too much rode on this.

'If I think the arrangement appropriate then who's to say otherwise?'

'Are you perverse with everyone or just me?' She spoke slowly, enunciating each syllable with clipped precision. 'I can't live in your home.'

'Is it your privacy you're concerned about? Are you worried I'll invade your space?'

The paparazzi labelled him a playboy because he wasn't seen with the same woman twice. No one knew that was due to boredom and a dislike of being the object of any greedy woman's avarice. These days his reputation for carnal pleasure owed everything to the fantasies of those he *hadn't* taken to bed. He hadn't desired a woman in years.

They always wanted something from him. Always had.

He hated how that made him feel.

Surely Lily Nolan didn't think he was so desperate he'd sexually harass his staff?

'The guest wing is separate, with its own entrance. There's a lock on the door connecting to the rest of the penthouse so you'll be quite alone.' In light of experience, *he* should be worried about *her* intruding.

Yet she remained silent. Indignation rose.

The sensation made him pause. Raffa couldn't remember the last time he'd felt it.

Because he always got his own way?

Or because there was little except business that he cared about, including what people thought of him?

'The arrangement is temporary. My PA had organised accommodation but there was trouble with burst pipes yesterday. The place is badly water damaged.'

'I could stay at a hotel.'

'You could, but you said you couldn't afford that. Something about spending your salary on other things.'

Her eyebrows lifted as if she recognised his curiosity and was surprised by it.

Dannazione! He was surprised by it!

'You couldn't have put me up somewhere else?'

'Because I'm rolling in cash?' She had a point. It would have been the work of a moment for Pete to make alternative arrangements. But Raffa was already financing her New York stay in style. Besides, having her close meant a chance to satisfy his curiosity.

'I didn't get rich by wasting money, Ms Nolan. The guest suite is empty and convenient for your work here. I can be sure you'll be on hand, doing what I want you to do, not off sightseeing.'

For a moment her eyes glowed and he could have sworn the temperature in the room rose a couple of degrees. But her temper didn't ignite. She really had phenomenal control.

Raffa refused to consider why he enjoyed testing it.

'You may recall I didn't want to come to New York. If you're concerned I'll get distracted I could go home and work there.'

He shook his head. 'You'll stay where you are till the other apartment is ready. I'm paying top dollar for your services. I want to be sure I get my money's worth.'

'You don't trust me?' Her head angled as if to view him better.

'I don't trust anyone till they prove themselves.'

Her gaze sharpened. 'You were the one eager to have me here.'

He shrugged and steepled his hands, elbows on the arms of his chair.

'Based on past performance, I judge you to be the person I need. But this project is more important than any you've done. Nothing will be left to chance.'

Lily looked into those bright blue eyes, felt the intensity of that searing stare and knew they'd reached the heart of things.

She felt the change in him. The quickening, the sizzle of energy.

Their conversation up to now had been skirmishes. Maybe he kept all new staff on their toes till he was convinced of their worth. Though why he'd take such a personal interest in her she couldn't fathom.

'Why is it so important?'

The furrow on his tanned brow disappeared as he leaned back. 'I won't brook failure on this.'

As far as Lily knew he never failed. Raffaele Petri had a nose for a good deal and a reputation for success. He also had an unerring instinct for what would appeal to the wealthiest clientele. That was how he'd built his fortune, with elite resorts, clubs and now marinas servicing those who demanded the best in everything. The rich always had enough to spend on themselves despite economic downturns that affected people like her, struggling to make a go of things.

'This man I'm to focus on, Robert Bradshaw...'

'Yes?'

'Can you tell me about him?'

'That's your job. I want a full report—his business interests, friends and connections. Everything.' Raffaele

Petri's expression didn't alter but Lily heard something in his voice that made the hair at her nape rise.

She had the disquieting certainty she was venturing into dangerous waters. Once more instinct yelled at her to back out. But she had no choice. He'd destroy her reputation if she reneged on this job.

'It would help if you told me something about the project.'

He regarded her, unblinking, and she shivered. It was said Raffaele Petri could seduce a woman with a glance from those stunning ocean-blue eyes. Not that he'd ever turn his fabled seduction skills on her. But what she read there now was hard calculation. Shrewdness as if he assessed her, deciding how much to share.

Not much, if the firm set of his sculpted jaw was an indication.

Lily stared back, trying to ignore the tremor of feminine response fluttering through her belly and the teasing trickle of heat in her blood.

What a time for her hormones to wake up from hibernation!

She breathed deep, corralling her thoughts. 'My other commissions for you have been to research companies or commercial trends, even localities.' They had been to determine if a site or company would be a good investment. 'This time it's about a man.'

Still he said nothing, as if waiting to see how far she could go connecting the dots.

Exasperation rose. 'Is there a particular angle I'm to focus on?'

'I told you. Everything. The size and nature of his income. His business associates. His interests, his weaknesses and habits. Who he sleeps with. The lot.'

Was it imagination, or did that stare harden?

She didn't imagine it. His voice when he'd said 'who he sleeps with' was different, his Italian accent stronger, like rich chocolate coating a lethal stiletto blade. She fought to repress a shiver. Whoever Robert Bradshaw was, whatever he'd done, she'd hate to be in his shoes.

In that instant Lily felt what she'd understood only intellectually before: Raffaele Petri would be a dangerous enemy.

Just as well she was too insignificant to be his enemy.

'I see.' She didn't, but clearly he wasn't going to enlighten her. 'Okay. I'll do the best I can.'

'That's not good enough. I need to know you'll deliver the goods.'

'You'll get your report, Signor Petri. But it will take time. This is a broad brief.' She waved one hand, trying to look brisk and organised, despite the chill sinking between her shoulder blades. 'His commercial interests and associates I can uncover. I'll do a thorough check on all those. His property and lifestyle, ditto. But there are limits.'

'Limits?' Dark eyebrows rose as if he'd never heard the word.

'I'm a researcher, Signor Petri, not a private detective. If you want information on this man's personal life, you'd do better hiring one of those. They can stake out his residence and give you an account of his comings and goings.'

He was already shaking his head. 'I learned long ago not to trust them. I want results, not excuses.'

Surprised, Lily leaned forward, then froze as she registered a warm, spicy scent. It teased her nostrils, sending shockwaves of delight to her belly.

It made her think of photos she'd seen of this man years ago. He'd lain half naked on a rumpled bed, jaw shadowed and his arms raised behind his head in a pose that accentuated the impressive musculature of his chest and arms. The sight had coaxed millions of women to buy decadently expensive aftershave for their men.

Was that what she smelled now? Lily inhaled, wondering at the art of producing a fragrance that seemed so purely natural, like hot male flesh and forbidden longing.

Abruptly she pulled back, trying to remember her train of thought.

That was it. When had he used private detectives in the past, and why didn't he like them?

His expression made it clear he wouldn't answer.

She shrugged. 'It's up to you. I'm just warning you that there are limits to my capabilities.'

'Yet you once worked in a private detection firm, even received some training.'

Lily stared. He knew *that* about her? She tried to recall how much detail she'd included on her résumé, but what really surprised her was that he'd read it personally.

'It was a long time ago and I didn't qualify as a private investigator. The work didn't suit me.' She'd got sick of grubbing around in people's personal lives. Commercial research was much less seedy.

'But you have the skills. I want everything, from Bradshaw's finances to his phone records.'

Lily laid her hands in her lap, maintaining her aura of calm despite the alarm bells going off in her head.

'Unless you have a warrant, phone records are protected.' She paused, breathing deep. 'Obviously you're not talking about hacking into phone company records.'

Those straight, decisive eyebrows rose. 'Aren't I? But I understood you included hacking in your skill set.'

Lily reared back, her seat sliding away from the conference table. 'How did you know that? It was years ago.'

Her breath came in staccato bursts. It had been years since anyone had mentioned her one brush with the law. She'd been just a kid, bored from being alone so much, cut off from her friends by the regime of medical treatment and surgery she'd undergone. And by the fact that to a lot of her schoolmates she'd become a freak. Not just because of her scars, but because she'd been the one to survive. She'd wondered if they felt guilty because secretly they'd have preferred it if her popular friend Rachel had lived, not her.

Emotion tugged at her like an ocean current, threatening to pull her under.

Instead she focused on Raffaele Petri—so strong and arrogant and utterly in control. She'd bet he'd never felt overwhelmed or insecure. Surprisingly, that worked. Her racing pulse slowed.

'I chose the best for this project team, with the best skill set. Your short-lived career as a hacker was impressive. It's a wonder you got off so lightly.'

Lily crossed her arms over her chest. 'I was underage. And I did no damage.'

'No, just managed to break into one of the best protected and encrypted government databases in the world.'

'If you hired me to break the law, think again, Signor Petri. I won't do that for any client.' She sprang to her feet and paced away.

That was better. At last he read something definite in Lily Nolan. Not just anger but indignation and surely a little fear?

He didn't want to scare her. But she'd sparred with him for so long he'd begun to wonder what it would take to probe past her control. Even when she was angry she'd been coolly poised, a challenge, a mystery he couldn't resist prodding.

Not now. Now Raffa saw the woman behind the mask of calm self-sufficiency.

What he saw heightened his interest.

Lily Nolan's eyes flashed fire as she turned to face him. Her lips moved in what he was sure was an unconscious pout of defiance. A pout any red-blooded man would respond to.

Except he was her boss.

He never harassed his staff.

Besides, he wasn't into kissing. He'd perfected the art from necessity but never really enjoyed it. It was a tool like any other to get what he wanted.

Raffa stilled, surprised at his blurring thoughts. He didn't want to kiss Lily Nolan. The idea was farcical.

He wanted to understand her. Label and catalogue her so she no longer took up even a scintilla of his brain space. Then he'd move on to more important things.

Yet now he'd provoked a reaction he wanted more. Contempt welled. Had he turned into what he'd always abhorred? A wealthy man so self-absorbed his only delight was toying with others?

'You have scruples, Ms Nolan.'

She strode back to stand close, hands on her hips.

'There are lines I won't cross, Signor Petri. Breaking the law is one.'

Spoken like a woman who'd never experienced real need. Raffa's mouth tightened. He knew precisely the depths to which poverty and desperation could drive people.

Or was that the excuse he used to justify his past?

'Not even for money?'

Those eyes weren't muddy brown now. They looked almost pure amber, rimmed with honey brown, and they met his with quiet certainty. 'Not even for money.'

Slowly he nodded. 'Good. Then presumably you can't be bought by a competitor to betray confidential information.'

A furrow appeared on her forehead. 'Was all this some elaborate test of my honesty?'

Raffa shrugged. Easier to let her believe his interest was so straightforward than try to explain something he didn't understand himself.

If her report was insufficient, he'd have to ignore his prejudice and hire a detective. At least now he wouldn't be sucked in by nebulous 'promising leads' that required just a little more time to produce results.

Years ago, when he'd begun making decent money, he'd

spent lavishly on fruitless investigations. Older than his years in most ways, his desperation to find the man responsible for his sister's death had made him gullible in this one area.

Now he knew better. He didn't trust investigators.

He didn't trust anyone.

Raffa pushed his chair back and stood. 'We'll meet when you've completed your initial report.'

By that time this fascination would have worn off. She'd be just another employee.

CHAPTER FOUR

THERE WAS NO SOUND, no disturbance, but suddenly Lily knew she was no longer alone.

Her spine tingled from her scalp to her tailbone. Her skin drew tight and she realised she'd frozen, fingers on the keyboard, waiting.

Slowly she lifted her head.

There he was, one shoulder propped against the door-jamb, legs casually crossed at the ankles. The only man whose presence she could sense with unerring accuracy.

Every time.

Even before he looked at her.

Even when he never looked at her.

It was a sixth sense, something primitive, buried so deep in her animal instinct as to be inexplicable. Yet it happened whenever Raffaele Petri got near. Lily was always the first to notice his presence. Her senses were on alert when he was nearby, even if he wasn't talking to her.

Now he watched her with a heavy-lidded look that made her blood surge.

She'd thought him stunning in the casual trousers and jackets he wore in the office. But in formal clothes... Her eyes widened. He looked like some sinfully gorgeous fallen angel wearing a tuxedo and a lazy half smile. The bow tie loose around his collar added a decadently raffish air.

'Working late again?'

Lily nodded and cleared her throat. Ridiculous that he had this effect after more than a month, but there was no mistaking the excited pump of her heart or that sudden breathlessness.

It did no good to tell herself millions of other women

had the same reaction. Or that she made a fool of herself. All she could do was ensure no one, most especially the man before her, guessed.

'But obviously not to impress the boss.' He crossed his arms but Lily kept her eyes on his face, refusing to dwell on the way the gesture emphasised the impressive symmetry of his broad-shouldered, slim-hipped frame.

'You think not?' Her voice worked after all.

What she'd give for an interruption! These days other members of staff were in and out of her office regularly. To her surprise, after their initial shock they'd accepted her as one of the team—so different from her other work experiences. Maybe because she'd been so focused on this project she hadn't had the leisure to stress about their reactions?

Yet a frantic glance through the glass walls told her they were alone. Everyone had gone home long ago.

'I know not.' He straightened and, to her alarm, stepped into her office.

'You're a mind-reader now too?' The words blurted out.

'In addition to what?' He stopped a couple of paces from her desk, sucking all the oxygen out of her office. 'No, don't tell me. I'll enjoy the challenge of working it out.'

Lily sat back, letting her hands drop to her lap. His words were light, as if he viewed their interactions as some sort of game.

Well, she wasn't playing.

Especially since his light tone didn't match that assessing scrutiny.

'How do you know I'm not trying to impress you with my diligence?' Better to stick to concrete issues than try to guess what was going on in that brilliant, convoluted mind.

He shrugged, the fluid movement innately Italian.

'You never look to me for approval. You don't hang about my office asking questions or showing off your success with what you've unearthed about Bradshaw.'

Lily's mouth twitched, a smile hovering at the implication he'd been impressed. But she was too much on edge to allow her lips to curve up. If she let down her guard with this man, she sensed she might never be able to resurrect it.

No matter how charming he could be, Raffaele Petri was dangerous. He'd forced her here. He'd unleashed a sexual awareness in her that terrified her. Every day and every night he'd loomed in her thoughts, a forbidden temptation when she should have been focusing on work or sleep or anything but mortifyingly sensual imaginings.

'You see the end results anyway.' Carefully she laced her fingers together as if relaxed. 'What would be the point of hanging around your office showing off every little success?'

Those sculpted lips stretched in a smile that tugged a sexy crease down one tanned cheek.

Heat drilled from Lily's lungs to her belly, cramping her abdominal muscles and stirring sexual arousal, instant and unmistakable.

That was why she needed to be vigilant. Raffaele Petri didn't just have the power to make or break her. He made her crave things that were impossible.

'You're paying for the best.' It had taken her a long time to develop self-confidence about her work and she refused to play coy about something that meant so much. 'I'm not so needy I require a pat on the head every time I do well.'

If she'd aimed to deflect his attention she'd erred. Instead of backing off, he surveyed her through narrowed eyes.

'Sometimes it's not about a pat on the head,' he murmured. 'Sometimes people just want my attention.'

Lily looked up into that bright, deliberate gaze, sifting his words.

Seeking attention.

From him.

Why? As soon as she asked the question she had the answer. Because they were attracted to him. Because they wanted him to notice them, respond to them. Just as a tiny, unstoppable part of her had fantasised he might—

She moved so abruptly her chair slid back from the desk, rolling till it crashed into the wall.

Lily found herself standing, her stomach churning so hard she tasted bile. He'd touched too close to her own secret desires and made them seem all the more pathetic. As if he suspected the attraction she couldn't quell.

Her right hand lifted in that old, compulsive gesture she'd taken years to vanquish. At the last moment, just before her fingers reached her scarred face, she remembered, forcing it back down, planting both palms on her desk. Her hands were damp against the wood, her throat jammed with distress.

It wasn't just that Raffaele Petri would never find her attractive. No man would.

She was experienced enough to accept that, after several painful experiences where she'd tentatively reached out to a man and had to endure horrified, embarrassed rejection. Yet some foolish part of her still fantasised.

It wasn't him she was angry with, but herself.

'You mean they want you to notice them because they're attracted to you?' Her voice was raw, stretched tight.

'It's been known to happen.' Again that fluid shrug, but she was beyond noticing how appealing it was. She was too caught up with the burn of shame and self-consciousness.

'You're annoyed I haven't fallen over myself to get your attention?' She almost choked on the words. Pride was her only lifeline and she clung to it tenaciously. 'You do realise there are some people who aren't bowled over by your beauty, Signor Petri?' Her tone made it clear she was one of them.

If only that were true! Daily exposure to Raffaele Petri had done nothing to inoculate her against his golden good looks. Instead it had given her a respect for his incisive decision-making and his ability to get the best out of his team. She'd discerned fairness and even a self-deprecating humour she found far too appealing.

The sound of laughter sliced her thoughts. Rich and warm, it encircled her like a caress. There was nothing calculated about it, or about his expression, and Lily had the impression that for a moment she saw Raffaele Petri as few did. For, despite his approachability to his staff, he usually exuded a sense of being utterly self-contained.

'You're absolutely right, Lily.' Her pulse gave a throb of pleasure at the sound of her name in that deep, lush voice. 'And an antidote to my overblown ego. Not everyone finds me attractive. It's good to know you're one of them. It makes working together much simpler.'

Lily breathed out slowly. Had she really fooled him? Maybe all those years masking her feelings and learning not to show vulnerability had stood her in good stead.

'What is it you want from me?' He hadn't singled her out again since her first day in the office, yet she hadn't been able to shake the feeling he noticed her almost as much as she did him. That he was aware of her, even when his attention was on something else. Not that he was attracted to her, of course, just assessing.

'Honestly?' Eyes of searing blue met hers and heat feathered her skin. 'I find you…interesting. Different.'

She snorted. This time she didn't stop her hand as it rose to her face. But, instead of touching scarred flesh, she deliberately pushed her hair back, tucking it behind her ear, revealing the whole marred side of her face.

Her chin angled higher as her gaze challenged his, defiant. 'Oh, I'm definitely different.'

'You think I'm talking about looks?' His eyebrows flattened in something close to a scowl.

It was her turn to shrug stiff shoulders. The movement had none of his beautiful fluidity. 'What else?'

He shook his head. 'I don't know.' For a moment he

looked almost perplexed. 'But it's got nothing to do with the way you look.'

Lily didn't know whether to be relieved or ridiculously hurt.

'Perhaps it's because I don't beat a path to your door.'

His eyebrows rose. 'If you had your way we'd be a hemisphere apart.'

Lily crossed her arms, projecting an ease she didn't feel. 'You're too used to people chasing you.'

'You think this is about ego?' He paused as if considering. 'Perhaps. But it's more too. I like the lateral way you think. The combination of solid, thorough research and inspired leaps of imagination. I saw it in your report on the Tahitian project and the ones since.'

Lily felt her strain ease, her muscles loosening. Professional accolades she'd accept gratefully. It was when they veered off work that discomfort grabbed her.

'I like that you're not afraid to voice your opinions.'

'I don't see any yes-men on your team.'

'Ah, but you take your independence to a fascinating new level. It's obviously a point of honour.'

'There's nothing special about me, Signor Petri. I'm merely a professional, used to being self-employed rather than having a boss.'

For too long he regarded her with that steady gaze she suspected saw too much.

'Maybe you're right.' He lifted his hands, closing the collar of his formal shirt then deftly tying the black satin bow tie.

Lily watched, fascinated to realise such a process could be so enthralling. Not just the fact he managed a bow tie with impressive ease and without a mirror, but that the action should be almost…arousing.

'Lily?'

She blinked. 'Yes?'

'I asked if it's straight.'

'Almost, just at a slight angle.'

'This way?' He twitched the black silk and she shook her head. 'Well?' An expressive eyebrow lifted. 'Can you help?'

She looked at the tie, askew against snowy linen and golden flesh, and felt something drop in her belly. She didn't want to touch Raffaele Petri. She didn't want to go near him.

But refusing wasn't an option. Briskly she stepped around the desk. She was close enough to inhale his signature scent of rich spices and warm male skin. That warmth enveloped her as she reached out and twitched his bow tie into place.

'There.' She kept her gaze fixed below his chin, ignoring her wobbly knees and the curious hollow sensation in her chest as if someone had scooped out all the air. 'Enjoy your evening out.' Then she turned back to her seat and her work.

It was only eleven-thirty when Raffa got home. Tonight's function had been more cloying than usual. His companion had pretended there was more to their night out than the mutual convenience of being seen with a suitable partner.

He strode through the living room, not bothering with lights. Moonlight streaming in made it easy to see the single bottle on the bar. Moments later he tossed back a mouthful of grappa, its heat punching through his impatience.

He was sick of the posturing and pretence, being part of the same well-heeled crew trying so hard to enjoy themselves. But he'd hoped to see Robert Bradshaw so he'd forced himself, pretending he gave a damn for 'society.'

Since he'd identified the man responsible for Gabriella's death he itched to bring him down. He had no hope of proving Bradshaw's guilt in court after all this time, but he'd see the man who'd seduced and discarded his sister utterly ruined.

But Bradshaw hadn't been there, probably nervous about facing so many creditors. Given the information Lily had unearthed, Raffa suspected he'd gone to ground on his private island, the one his family had owned since they'd traded in slaves and sugar. His homes in London and Cannes had been sold to pay debts and the New York apartment was next. No doubt he was licking his wounds, scheming how to recoup the fortune he'd inherited and squandered.

Raffa's fingers tightened on his glass as anticipation rose. It was time to take the game to Bradshaw. The decision lightened Raffa's mood. He'd grind Bradshaw into the dirt and enjoy every moment.

Discarding tie, shoes and socks, then yanking the top buttons of his shirt undone, he slid open the door to his roof terrace and stepped out. Raffa turned his face to the light breeze and stalled mid-step.

He wasn't alone.

Someone sat on a sun lounger by the pool. Someone staring not at the garden, or the Manhattan view, but the glowing screen of a laptop.

What was *she* doing here?

It had to be Lily Nolan. No one could get past security to his private space, except the woman in his guest suite. The woman who drew the curtains as soon as she got in each night to shut herself off. He'd wondered if she was agoraphobic. That might have explained her reluctance to come to New York. But here she was, with the city laid out before her, relaxed as if her eyrie position didn't bother her in the least.

So it wasn't the view she'd been shutting out, but him— her only neighbour on the penthouse level.

Intriguing.

A now familiar trickle of heat spilled through his veins. A sensation he felt whenever Lily Nolan interrupted his thoughts. He still hadn't found a name for it. Not arousal

or excitement. Nor mere curiosity. More a charged awareness, as if he waited for…

Raffa shook his head. He wasn't waiting for anything
from Ms Nolan, except another report, this time detailing
Bradshaw's Caribbean island resort built around an old
plantation estate.

She didn't hear him approach—was too absorbed in
what she was doing. Surely not work at this time?

What he saw fascinated him. For the first time she didn't
wear loose trousers and a shirt buttoned to the throat. Her
feet and legs were bare. His gaze travelled along lissom
thighs and shapely calves as she sat with legs bent to support her laptop. Her arms and shoulders were bare too and
free of scar tissue.

He'd wondered if she carried more scars under her long
sleeves and trousers. The thump of his pulse felt like relief
that her injuries weren't worse.

Her swathe of long hair was tucked back. She wore a
tank top and shorts and looked potently alluring.

Every woman he met projected an image—sophisticated, provocative, flirtatious, or brisk and professional.
Raffa halted, enjoying the silvery light on her naked limbs,
relishing the tantalising charm of a sexy woman who wasn't
deliberately projecting anything.

Raffa felt a sharp, unmistakable tug of response low
in his groin.

It was almost eclipsed by the quake of shock that ripped
through him an instant later, making his eyes widen and
his belly clench.

How long since he'd felt sexual arousal?

It seemed a lifetime since the thought of sex made him
feel anything but impatient or…tainted. For all its transient
pleasure, and Raffa had known plenty of that, sex was a
transaction, intimacy a calculated risk.

He frowned, his gaze stuck on Lily Nolan and the innocent simplicity of her sex appeal.

Even when he was young there'd never been anything innocent about sex. Simple, yes. But never innocent.

His gaze swept from her hair, dark in the moonlight, to her marred cheek, delicate throat and long limbs. The tug of awareness sharpened to coiling, gut-grabbing tension.

He'd thought he didn't give a damn what Lily Nolan looked like. He'd been wrong.

It was true her scar meant nothing to him. What difference could that make when even the most glamorous beauty failed to stir him? Yet the sight of Lily's supple bare limbs, her ripe breasts and delicate collarbone…

But it wasn't merely that she had a sexy body. He'd seen more than his share of those.

His response was as much to do with the fact that this was Lily Nolan. The woman who'd defied, intrigued and surprised him for six weeks. Even before that, when they'd spoken on the phone, there'd been something, a fizz of energy in his veins that made him feel different—more *alive*. More *real*.

Raffa's frown became a scowl. He didn't do flights of fancy or self-doubt.

Yet he'd always been honest with himself. It had been the only way to keep his head on the tumultuous ride from poverty to success, from obscurity to being one of the most recognisable men on the planet.

Which was why he accepted that it was, remarkably, desire weighting his lower body, sexual interest spiking for the first time in years. More important—it wasn't a reaction merely to an appealing body but specifically to Lily Nolan.

He drew a sharp breath as heat stabbed, keen as a blade.

She must have heard his indrawn breath, swinging her head around and stiffening, hands grabbing the computer.

'You!'

Raffa's mouth twisted wryly. 'Don't sound so pleased to see me.'

Lily Nolan was guaranteed to keep him grounded. Far

from falling at his feet, she viewed him as a necessary encumbrance.

If he believed in good triumphing over evil, in redemption, he'd be tempted to think she'd come into his life to save him, from his ego if nothing else.

But it was a lifetime since Raffa had believed in anything but himself.

'It *is* my home.' His gesture encompassed the garden and penthouse.

'But you went out.' She snapped her mouth shut as if to prevent more words bursting free.

'I see. That's why you sneaked out here. You thought I'd be out of the way.'

Predictably her jaw angled up. 'I didn't sneak anywhere. You told me I had access to the garden.'

'A privilege you've never used unless you believed me safely gone.' He paused, watching her compose her face, wiping away the signs of shock and replacing them with her habitual mask of composure. It annoyed him to realise how much he wanted to peer beyond that facade.

'I thought you'd appreciate privacy. Especially in the evening when you might be…entertaining.' She looked beyond him towards the door to the penthouse.

'Thoughtful of you,' he murmured, 'but unnecessary.' He didn't explain that he never *entertained* at home. He valued his privacy too much.

Besides, the memory of the permanently drawn curtains in the guest wing spoke not so much of giving him privacy but herself. Why did Lily Nolan conceal herself? What secret did she protect?

How hard would it be to unravel that protective web she'd woven around herself? To discover the Lily Nolan who warded him off with her fierce concentration on work? He hadn't missed how she removed herself from his company when possible. How she kept her distance, calling him *Signor Petri* when others used first names.

Tonight he'd get answers.

'What are you working on?' Maybe she'd surprise him and reveal she spent her evenings playing online games.

Her hand went out as if to close her laptop, but his hand shot out, covering hers.

Raffa's pulse throbbed hard. He'd only touched her once, the day they'd shaken hands, but strangely there was a beckoning familiarity to her smooth flesh beneath his.

A second later her fingers slid away and she sat, cradling her hand as if stung.

Interesting.

And far more convenient to concentrate on her reaction than his own.

Raffa angled the screen to see it better. 'Consumer buying patterns in Brisbane? What's that got to do with Bradshaw? I wasn't aware he had interests there.'

'He doesn't.' The screen was pulled from his grip and closed. 'This work isn't for you.'

'You're moonlighting?' She was so close he inhaled that delicate scent he'd noticed before. Subtle yet sweet. It reminded him of crisp, cool days and...pears? That was it—ripe, luscious pears.

She shifted away, further down the lounge seat. Did she somehow register the abrupt spike of adrenaline flooding his bloodstream? The sharpening of his senses now she was within touching distance.

Raffa applauded her good sense in moving.

Yet he grabbed another chair and hauled it over, sitting so he faced her, knee to knee.

Playing safe had never been his style.

CHAPTER FIVE

LILY FOLDED THE laptop on her knees as if it might protect her from his keen gaze.

She felt vulnerable out here, away from the office. Away from her clothes! With that thought her nipples tightened into needy pebbles against the cotton of her sleep top.

How long before her body stopped responding to this man as a virile, spectacular male? She longed for the day she could relegate him to a mere colleague like the ones she worked with daily. The ones who, to her surprise, were becoming friends.

Lily swallowed a groan. Caught half naked by Raffaele Petri. Thankfully he hadn't turned on the lights.

Not that he needed lights. The moon was bright. Enough for her to have difficulty keeping her gaze off the tantalising V of skin revealed by his partly unbuttoned shirt. The combination of formal clothes and rumpled hair, bare feet and open shirt made him look even more potently masculine than usual. Every nerve centre relayed shock waves of pleasure at the sight.

How could her body betray her so?

'Moonlighting implies I'm going behind your back,' she snapped, stress tightening her vocal chords. 'That I'm cutting corners on my work for you. That's not so.' Better to focus on that than her body's tingling excitement.

'So what *are* you doing?'

She drew a deep breath, marshalling her thoughts, and was surprised to intercept a flicker of movement as his gaze dropped to her chest. Instantly her nipples budded tighter as if trying to push closer to him.

Lily told herself it was a reaction to the breeze.

'I told you I had responsibilities that meant I couldn't come to New York, but you forced my hand. This—' she waved a hand at the laptop '—is one of them. A job for a business looking to expand in Brisbane. I was checking a draft report from my assistant.'

'Assistant? I thought you worked alone?'

Once more Lily was unsettled that Raffaele Petri had taken time to learn about her.

'I recently expanded my business. There's a good market for high-quality research.' He said nothing and she felt compelled to fill the silence. 'I'm not cutting corners on your work. I'm doing this in my own time.'

'At midnight? That's no way to run a business.'

It stung that he of all people should lecture on her gruelling work schedule. As if her exhaustion didn't remind her every day when she dragged herself out of bed, almost drip feeding coffee to keep going.

'You think I don't know that?' She shook her head, finally breaking free of his gaze and turning to look over the diamond-sprinkled velvet of the city at night. Even now, with Raffaele Petri evoking desires she had no business feeling, she couldn't quite get over the fact she was *here*, in New York, the city she'd never believed she'd visit. What wouldn't she give for a chance to explore? To wander and be part of the anonymous crowd? Yet, despite her growing ease with her colleagues, that was a step too far.

'I don't have a choice. Not since I was blackmailed into coming here despite my other work commitments.'

'*That's* why you were reluctant to leave? Not because of a man?'

Lily almost snorted in derision. A man? That was a laugh. There'd been no men in her life. They weren't exactly lining up outside her door, besotted by her looks and charm. Not even when she'd been fourteen and fresh-faced had she been that popular with boys. She'd been too ordinary, too easily overlooked. And later she was noticed for

the wrong reasons. She'd learned the hard way not to con-
fuse sympathy for interest.

'Several men, actually.' She watched, surprised, as he
stiffened. Was it imagination or did his eyes narrow? 'That
retailer in Brisbane. The HR manager of a security firm
wanting checks on potential staff. The head of a planning
authority—'

'Clients, you mean.'

'Yes. And all important. Which is why I use my spare
time working for them.'

'But none are as important as me.'

True. None had the same power to make or break her
business.

'*All* my clients are important. They expect results and
I'd already promised to deliver. I don't take on work I can't
complete to the best possible standard.'

'Even if the projects bring in a pittance compared with
what you're doing for me?'

Lily tried not to grind her teeth. Good thing he was
so arrogant. It would counteract this powerful attraction.

Shame it hadn't worked yet.

'You'd be surprised. Some of my clients even rival you.'
She'd recently done work for a man who could reasonably
be called Raffaele Petri's rival. Luca De Laurentis was another entrepreneur providing vacation services to the rich.
'For my business to expand it makes sense to cultivate as
many sources of income as possible.'

Slowly—perhaps reluctantly?—he nodded.

'When you say expand, what do you mean? There's only
so much you can do, even if you go without sleep.'

'Is it so hard to take me seriously as a businesswoman?
To see me as an employer?' Umbrage thickened her voice.
Her work, her professional success, meant everything. They
were all she had. She'd long ago realised she'd never have
a family of her own.

He shook his head. 'You're the most serious-minded

person I know, Lily.' Inevitably there it was again, the tiny thrill of delight as he turned her name into something exotic with that mellow voice and mouthwatering accent. 'It's just that you obviously prefer to work alone.'

'You mean I'm not a team player?' She read criticism in his words.

'No, not that. I've seen how meticulous you are about sharing information, making sure everyone's up-to-date. More that you prefer to be alone.'

Lily swallowed, her throat tight. He was right. Over the years she'd developed a taste for her own company. Surely he could understand that.

Or maybe not. People stared at him all the time, but it was in admiration, not horror at how he looked.

'Well, you'll be interested to know I employ two other people.' Albeit part-time, and both still learning the ropes. But for Lily this was a major step forward.

'Why?'

She frowned. Hadn't he listened? 'You said yourself there's a limit to the work I can do alone.'

'Why expand? Why build up a company rather than accept a permanent job here, for instance?' His voice resonated with genuine curiosity.

Lily stared into that gorgeous fallen-angel face. No one else, not her family or friends or even her bank manager, had bothered to ask.

Something faltered inside her. She found herself on her feet, staring at the beautifully lit pool. Yet she couldn't distract herself from stirring disquiet. Her heart thumped high in her chest and she knew it was because his interest made a difference. What he thought mattered.

Despite their differences she respected him—his business acumen, his drive, even his sometimes brutal honesty. And the fact he'd never once seemed fazed by her looks. He treated her not as scarred Lily Nolan but, she realised in shock, as someone strong enough to stand up to him. As an equal, despite their imbalance of power.

She should end this conversation. It bordered on the intimate. Yet their isolation in this moon-washed garden and the sense of familiarity made it seem almost normal.

It struck her how far she'd cut herself off from those who cared about her. In Australia she'd crossed a continent to get away from her family's loving but claustrophobic over-protectiveness, moving from Fremantle, on the west coast, to the east. Since then she'd focused on work. She had no bosom buddy, no confidante. No one close to share her hopes and dreams.

'I want to build something for myself.' The words tumbled out.

To her surprise he nodded. Only a tiny inclination of the head but it seemed to bridge the distance between them.

'I want...' How did she put it into words? 'Security, the safety that comes from success, but more too. I want...'

'Recognition.'

Lily's eyes widened. 'How did you know?'

His shoulders lifted and her gaze slid across that wide, straight expanse of powerful muscle and bone. 'It sounds familiar.'

'You?' It didn't seem possible. 'But you already had recognition before you started your business.'

His lips curved in what should have been a smile.

'To be recognisable as a face, or a body, plastered across the media in advertising campaigns isn't quite the same as genuine recognition.'

'Recognition for your achievements, you mean?'

Again that nod.

Was it naive to admit she'd never thought of the difference before? Raffaele Petri's phenomenal media presence had seemed the epitome of success. To be so watched, adored and admired...

It was as if he'd read her mind. 'Being known because

of how you look isn't an achievement.' His eyes held hers and phantom heat washed her scarred face. 'Being someone because of your actions, your success, is something else.'

Understanding stretched between them. An understanding she'd never before shared. It felt momentous. Lily sank back onto her seat, watching him avidly.

'Is that what drove you to build your business? The need to make your mark?' She admired him for that. It would have been easy to continue modelling. To move from that field where he was in such demand and strike out on his own must have taken grit as well as talent.

'Maybe. I wanted to take charge of my future. That's hard when you're dependent on the whims of advertisers and fashion gurus, likely to be out of style next year because they're hungry for a new face.'

She blinked, astounded that he shared such information. He wasn't a touchy-feely sort of guy. She'd seen him affable and relaxed but he could as easily intimidate with a look.

Was he too affected by the intimacy of the half-darkness, high above the city?

'I can't imagine you out of modelling work for long.' It wasn't just his staggering good looks. He had a magnetism Lily couldn't resist, no matter how she tried. And she'd tried. For over a month she'd fought the compulsion to watch him.

He laughed, the sound a soft ripple skating along her bare arms. 'It's a cutthroat business. Don't let the gloss fool you.'

'So you took to real estate as a safety net?' That was how he'd started his enterprise.

'You could say that. I was determined to make myself safe.'

'Safe?'

Again that quirk of the lips that should have been a smile, but which felt, in the dimness, like something else.

'I was born poor. It takes a lot of money to stop worrying you'll lose everything and end up in the gutter again.'

Lily nodded. She knew he didn't come from money. But the gutter? Was that just a figure of speech?

'Building my business meant I could choose my direction, doing things the way I want, not dependent on others.'

'I know what you mean.'

He sat back, and even in the semi-darkness she felt his piercing regard.

Lily held her breath, waiting for him to continue. He didn't. He looked perfectly relaxed, watching her. But he sat closer than in any meeting. There was nothing between them except a few scant inches of space.

Abruptly the elusive feeling of companionship dissipated.

The silence grew and Lily's lungs tightened with the effort to breathe normally, not gulp down huge draughts of warm air, scented with that man and spicy deliciousness she'd come to associate with him.

'What are you thinking?' she burst out when she couldn't bear the silence.

His mouth quirked up again and this time she spied amusement. 'I'm thinking how similar we are.'

He had to be kidding! They were galaxies apart.

'We're both loners.' He ticked the point off one finger. Lily watched, fascinated that he lumped himself with her there. Raffaele Petri was always surrounded by people. In the office he was the hub around which everyone revolved, eager to meet his needs. She'd seen enough media reports to know that out of the office he was surrounded by glamorous, beautiful people, drawing them like a magnet.

But how many is he close to?

The question had never occurred to her before.

'We both want the security of success.' Another tick. 'We both want to make our mark, rather than have the world judge us on how we look.'

Lily sucked in her cheeks on a hiss of shock, blinking at those knowing eyes. She'd never mentioned the problem she'd had since her teens—of people not seeing her, just her scarred face.

It stunned her that he'd picked up on that.

Why had she thought he wouldn't get it? Because he wasn't interested in anyone but himself? Yet he'd continually surprised her with what he knew about her.

Because he was so handsome?

For the first time it struck her that he carried a burden too—far easier, of course, since his looks must have opened doors. In a weird way they were linked—judged by people because of their faces— his utterly gorgeous and hers downright ugly.

Slowly Lily released her breath, and with it some of the tautness in her shoulders and neck.

She nodded. He'd put into words something she'd never admitted. That she still fought to be judged as someone other than the woman with the appallingly scarred face.

That was why, until now, she'd enjoyed working from home instead of in someone else's office. When people couldn't see her they treated her like anyone else—no pity or sneaking stares or embarrassment.

Working here in New York was the first time in years she'd begun to relax with others. Were the people here remarkable or did her hard-won confidence in her work mean she was less concerned with their initial reaction? Whatever the cause, she felt more relaxed and accepted than she'd expected. It irked to admit it but her forced move had been good for her.

'We've both set up our own businesses too. That's another point in common.' It didn't matter that his was a multinational empire and hers a fledgling company carrying brand-new debt. The principle was the same. 'Did your previous career help you get started?'

His laugh was short. 'Not in the beginning. I wasn't

taken seriously. I was a face, not a businessman. No one understood how single-minded I'd had to be to get where I was.'

'I suppose people think modelling is easy.' She had.

'Modelling?' He shifted in his seat, his head swinging up, and she had a curious feeling she'd missed something. 'Let's just say I paid my dues to climb out of the hole where I started life.' His face hardened. 'Getting investors to trust me with their assets was tough. Everyone expected me to fail.'

'But you didn't.'

'In the beginning, when I needed advice and investors, no one would touch me. Later it was different. People wanted a part of what I'd built, but by then I was used to working alone.' He shrugged. 'Maybe being forced to go solo was a good thing. It made me more determined to succeed and learn from my mistakes.'

'Did you make many? Mistakes?' Lily leaned forward, her hands clasped between her knees.

'Plenty. I had money, I'd been careful about saving, but I overextended myself with a project that ran into problems. It was touch-and-go for a while.'

Lily knew the feeling. 'But you succeeded.' Fervently she hoped she could too.

He lifted one hand, palm up, in a gesture that seemed wholly Italian. 'It was the only option I'd accept.'

Didn't that say it all? Raffaele Petri was a man who, as Pete said, made it his policy always to get what he wanted. Did she have the same determination to succeed?

'You make it sound easy.'

'Not easy. Straightforward. I refused to accept failure. I did whatever it took to succeed.'

Could she do that? She was trying. How hard she was trying!

Perhaps it was ridiculous to take solace from the example of the man who'd disrupted her plans, the one forcing her to work twice as hard as usual just to keep on top of her obligations. Yet she felt buoyed.

'Have you considered narrowing your market?' His query dragged her out of her reverie.

'Sorry?'

'Your market. It seems very broad. You're doing personnel security checks. You've taken a job for a small business plus some project for a planning authority. Then there's your work for me, which is in a different ballpark. I'm asking if you need to specialise and become the best at what you do instead of being all things to all people.'

Lily surveyed him with surprise. Instead of anger that she wasn't devoting all her efforts to his project, he was interested in her business? Offering advice? It was too good an opportunity to ignore.

'Specialising would cut off some lucrative income.' Like those security checks she didn't particularly enjoy.

'Lucrative long-term or short-term?'

She hadn't thought about it like that. 'Lucrative enough to pay the bills while I build my name in the areas I want.'

'And do you have a plan for the transition from doing everything to doing only what you want as your core business?'

Lily hesitated. Her business plan had been based on doing more of the same. General expansion rather than targeted. Her focus had been on building income to make the enterprise as secure as possible.

'I see.' He sat back.

So did she. 'There's a gap in my planning, isn't there?'

She didn't feel defensive. This shadowy version of Raffaele Petri, sitting easily with her in the garden, wasn't nearly as daunting as the one she worked with daily. She could almost pretend to forget her attraction to him. Despite her quickened pulse and the tingle of awareness, she felt easier with him than ever before. As if he were no longer a threat.

Amazing what a little moonlight could do. Or was it because his interest was in her work, not her?

'It sounds like you need to revisit your strategy. Unless you want to be stuck in a rut, tendering for every job, whether it interests you or not.'

Lily dragged her fingers through her hair, letting it slide away over her shoulder. 'I've had enough of that, working at things that don't interest me.'

Even in the moonlight she saw his eyebrows rise. 'Does that apply to what you're doing for me?'

Quickly Lily shook her head. 'No, I love that.' She paused, wondering if she sounded too eager. But he'd acknowledged she never ran to him seeking kudos. 'The projects are complex enough to be fascinating. I—' She paused. 'Signor P—'

'Raffaele. Or Raffa. Surely we've gone past formality.'

Lily wished his face wasn't half-shadowed. There was a note in his voice she couldn't recognise. It kicked her pulse into high gear.

Reluctantly she nodded. 'Raffaele.' She stumbled over his name. Not because she couldn't say it, but because it felt like an illicit pleasure on her tongue. As if she'd crossed some boundary. Heat spiked in her chest. 'Is there a chance you could…?'

'A chance I could…?' He leaned forward and she felt the waft of warm air as he exhaled. Lily blinked, overwhelmed by his sheer physical presence. The stark male beauty that even pale moonlight couldn't diminish. The challenging mind. The fizz of attraction.

Yet most appealing of all was the way he talked to her. He made her feel…important. As if she genuinely interested him.

Lily's gaze fell to those powerful hands at his knees. Her blood tingled as for one decadent moment she wondered how it would feel if he lifted a palm and put it on her bare flesh. A quiver of exultation coursed through her. Till sanity returned.

The very fact he was so close, discussing corporate planning of all things, proved he had no interest in her physically. It was her mind, her plans he was curious about.

She was glad. It was what she wanted, to be taken seriously as a businesswoman.

Yet Lily couldn't help wondering what it would be like, just once, to be desired by a man.

She gulped down a sudden restriction in her throat. She didn't do self-pity. Far better to focus on what she *could* get out of life.

'I wondered if you had any advice. About how or when to make that switch from taking every job to something more targeted.'

Her nerves stretched with the growing silence. But just when she'd decided she'd gone too far, he spoke.

Raffa watched Lily expound a point, gesturing, the light catching the small scar on the back of her hand. It caught the larger scar on her cheek too. But not even that detracted from her lit-from-within animation.

When she talked about her business it was with an enthusiasm most women reserved for a lover. An enthusiasm he found hard to resist.

True passion was rare.

How many would-be entrepreneurs had approached him to give them a start up? How many established businessmen had tried to entice him into a shared deal? He was adept at resisting, going his own way.

Yet here he was, caught up in Lily Nolan's enthusiasm for a solid, but nevertheless tiny enterprise.

Or, more accurately, caught up in watching her, enjoying the change from buttoned-up, defensive worker bee to a woman who even in this gloom shone with an inner glow. A woman who made him wonder what she'd do if he stretched his arm out and hauled her onto his lap.

Her effervescence was a turn-on. It was no hardship to discuss business plans with her. He'd been genuinely interested, but beyond that was an edge that had nothing to do with commerce and everything to do with the fact that for the first time in recent memory he found himself contemplating taking a lover.

Lily Nolan?

It was a crazy idea.

'When will that report on Bradshaw's Caribbean property be complete?'

She looked surprised at his question. Understandable given it had nothing to do with their discussion. 'Tomorrow. I've got one more thing to check in the morning.'

'Excellent. You can have ten days off when it's done. That will give you time to work through your other responsibilities.' He gestured to her now dormant laptop. The sooner she got on top of those, the sooner he could have her to himself. He needed her. For her expertise, he assured himself.

'Ten days? But I've only worked for you a short time.'

Raffa's mouth kicked up. Who complained about time off? 'Don't worry. I'm getting my money's worth from you and I intend to keep doing so. When you start back we'll be in a crucial stage of the project and I'll want you available twenty-four-seven.'

Slowly she nodded. 'Well, I *am* on the premises, so I'll be available.'

Raffa shook his head. 'We won't be in New York. We'll be in the Caribbean, on Bradshaw's home turf.'

She stilled, her eyes widening. 'We?'

'That's right. We. I want you where you can be most useful.'

This was a sensible business decision. It had nothing to

do with the tug of attraction he felt towards Lily Nolan.
Almost nothing.

She opened her mouth, the same tight expression settling on her face that he'd become used to before tonight.
It didn't bother him. Now he knew something of the vital,
intriguing, oddly innocent woman behind the façade.

He looked forward to seeing more of that woman. To
learning her secrets.

'And, before you object, this is a requirement, not a re-
quest. Finish what you have to. I don't want you bringing
other work. I want you completely at my disposal.'

CHAPTER SIX

'THAT'S IT FOR NOW. Thanks, everyone.' Raffaele ended the video conference with a final word to Consuela in New York about a contract.

Lily eased back in her seat, stretching. She was tired, but good tired. Working with Raffaele was intense—satisfying, but a challenge to keep up. Just as well she'd been well prepared for the meeting.

He was a dynamic entrepreneur but his restless energy since they'd arrived on Bradshaw's island was electric. There must be a personal element to this. She sensed it in the grim twist of Raffaele's mouth when the other man was mentioned, and his insistence on breakneck speed, as if completion couldn't come fast enough. Yet even now he was cagey about the details of his plan, as if it were too important to share in full.

'Right. Time for a break.'

She looked up to find he'd shut the screen and was watching her. His stare made her feel abruptly *un*professional.

Lily worked hard *not* to think of him as a desirable man. But it was like trying to pretend the sun didn't shine out there on the white sand of this island paradise. The mere sight of his sinewy, powerful forearms, dark gold beneath rolled-up sleeves, made her stupid heart thud.

They were alone in his spacious bungalow, set a little apart from the other accommodation spread through the leafy resort gardens. The rest of the team were thousands of miles away in New York and Lily felt a flicker of guilt that she alone had travelled here with him. Even her smaller bungalow was gorgeous, with its plantation-style furnishings, four-poster bed and ocean views.

'Dinner at the poolside café, I think.'

Lily could imagine him there. With his burnished good looks and casual white cotton shirt and trousers, he'd be right at home amongst the bikini-clad beauties.

She averted her gaze, gathering her gear. 'Enjoy yourself. I'll start following up—'

'Later, Lily. It's time to eat.' That mellow voice trailed through her veins.

She fixed on a smile. 'I'll grab something in my room. I want to get this down while it's fresh.'

To her surprise he came to stand before her, crossing his arms and planting his feet wide, owning the space.

Her pulse danced that silly little jig. No matter how often she saw him, he still had the power to enthral her. She should be immune to Raffaele Petri. But since that night on his rooftop her defences were in tatters.

He'd taken time to advise her on her fledgling enterprise. She'd never had a mentor and eagerly soaked up his suggestions. He'd been kind, discussing her insignificant start-up company.

Who'd have thought Raffaele Petri could be kind?

There'd been more too. He'd told her about his own business. For the first time she saw her research in a wider context. It was exciting to feel part of something bigger than her own narrow goals. He'd made her feel valued, as if she *belonged*. It was rare and satisfying.

Above all was the heady sense he saw her not just as an employee but as a woman interesting in her own right. He made her feel he saw *her* as no one else did. She was human enough to want him to admire what he saw.

'That can wait. Food first. Leave your stuff here and collect it later.'

He was inviting her to eat with him? Excitement buzzed.

Or was that horror at the thought of sitting at the resort's most public venue beside the most gorgeous man on the planet? With all those beautiful people looking on?

Her shrinking stomach warned it was both.

'Thanks, Raffaele.' She paused, savouring his name. 'But I'd prefer to eat alone and get my thoughts together.'

'In your room?'

She nodded, scrambling up from the low seat.

To her consternation he didn't step away and she found herself toe to toe with him, close enough for the heat of his body to brand her. For that evocative scent of his to inveigle its way into her nostrils.

Awareness shuddered through her—real, alive, all-consuming.

The daunting truth was that she wanted him as a woman wanted a man. It was laughable. He'd been supportive and, yes, kind, but there was no way he'd ever—

'Hiding again, Lily?'

Her chin tipped up as if yanked on a string. She met gleaming eyes and read knowledge in them. Her breath froze and splintered in her lungs.

'I don't know what you're talking about.' He couldn't know how she felt about him. Could he?

Raffa scented her fear. He'd learned to recognise it early, a legacy of growing up in the rough end of a derelict neighbourhood. He wanted to tell her it was okay.

But it wasn't okay, not if what he suspected was right. His hands clenched as he strove not to reach for her. The impulse to reassure, to comfort was so unexpected and strong, it shocked him.

He'd been many things to many women.

But a comfort? Never.

Yet he persisted. His suspicion had grown so strong he'd found himself pondering it rather than his plans for Bradshaw. Nothing, he vowed, would deter him from justice for Gabriella. For her sake, and for Lily's, he needed to sort this so he could focus again.

'We've worked together long enough for me to be able

to read you, at least a little.' He'd never met anyone so self-contained. It made him itch to discover her secrets. 'I know you're scared.'

She froze. He sensed the tightening of her slim frame as her eyebrows rose. 'I don't know what you mean.'

He gave her full marks for bravado.

'You think I haven't noticed that you hide away?' He shook his head. 'You never go out. Ever. In New York you stayed in the office or in the guest suite. When other staff talk about what they did on the weekend or meet for a drink after work, you don't join in.' He'd been too absorbed in his plan for justice to realise at first how insular she was. But, once he did, it was glaringly obvious. Like the way she concealed herself behind that long hair.

'You *know* I don't have time for that.' She waved a hand dismissively. 'I'm working full-time for you and trying to keep my business afloat back home.'

True, but that wasn't the whole story.

'You've got time to eat with me. Here. Now.' He paused. 'Unless you're afraid of that too?'

'Too?' Lily shifted as if to step away but he blocked her exit.

'I saw you on the beach at dawn.' At her surprised look he shrugged. 'You're not the only early riser.'

Instantly suspicion, or was it fear, clouded those amber-brown eyes.

'You were staring out to sea, even waded knee-deep in the water a couple of times. But you didn't go in. Why was that? I could tell you were yearning to.'

She'd stood there in another long-sleeved shirt with cargo pants rolled up around her knees and it had struck him how she deliberately camouflaged that lithe, luscious body he'd seen in his garden.

He'd been about to approach her when he'd noticed her expression, illuminated in the peachy morning light. It was a look of such longing, such regret, it stirred discomfort. As if he'd intruded on something utterly personal.

The melancholy of that lone figure, arms crossed over her chest, just as now, had stayed with him all morning.

'I wasn't *yearning*. I was admiring. The view was spectacular.' She hitched a quick breath that betrayed discomfort, her gaze skittering away. 'Besides, I didn't bring a swimsuit.'

'You came to a Caribbean resort and didn't bring a swimsuit?' Disbelief dripped from each syllable.

Her chin jerked even higher. 'I don't own one.' She hurried on before he could interrupt. 'I'm here to work, not swim, remember?'

'I see.' She was finding excuses again. More than ever, he wanted to lay them bare.

'What do you see?' Anger vibrated in her voice and Raffa felt a little of his edginess ease. He preferred her angry to fearful or dejected. Watching her this morning, reading infinite sadness in that longing gaze, had felt like a sucker punch to the gut. He'd felt…lost, something he hadn't experienced since he was twelve and Gabriella had left him.

'That you're afraid of the water. Can't you swim?'

'Of course I can swim. I grew up on the coast. Learning to swim was compulsory.'

Raffa stared at her set features, reading the truth in her expression. Now they were getting somewhere.

He lifted his hand, gesturing to her scarred cheek. 'What happened? Was that from an accident in the water? Is that why you don't swim?'

Lily gasped and shifted back but she couldn't escape because of the couch behind her.

'Lily?'

'That's none of your business.' Her voice rose half an octave.

'Perhaps not. But it's time someone asked.' Clearly her

injury had affected more than her face. It was a crying shame that a woman so full of spark and energy should conceal herself.

Why was he making it his mission to interfere?

He was selfish to the core. Since when had he taken an altruistic interest in anyone?

'Just because you employ me doesn't give you a right to pry.'

Raffa said nothing, merely stood and waited.

He'd almost given up on an answer when the words burst from her. 'It wasn't a swimming accident. A jealous thug decided to make a point with a flask of acid.'

Raffa recoiled at the brutal words. He couldn't help but imagine the fiery burn on tender flesh, the howling pain. The shock and suffering. Nausea swirled in his belly and rose as bile in his throat. His heart pounded his ribs.

What sort of man attacked a defenceless woman?

Another like Robert Bradshaw.

Raffa's hands curled into fists, tension radiating up his arms to his shoulders and neck.

'Your boyfriend?' His words slid from between gritted teeth.

She shook her head, her long hair slipping around her cheeks. 'My best friend's. I was just in the wrong place at the wrong time, sitting beside her at the cinema. Rachel bore the brunt of it but my injuries kept me in and out of hospital for a long time while they tried to repair the damage.' Her voice was brittle.

It struck him how tough it must have been, not only badly injured, but in such a random way. How had she ever felt safe again?

He wanted to soothe her, haul her close and reassure her.

As if he had any experience of comforting a woman.

As if she'd accept his touch! She glared at him with the same distrust he'd once seen on a half-wild dog. As if she'd bite his hand if he came close.

'So why don't you swim?' There was something there, some reason she wouldn't go in the water. He'd seen it on her face in the dawn light. 'Is it the same reason you try to disappear?'

'Disappear? I'm here, aren't I?' Her voice told him he was on the right track. Defiance tinged with fear.

'Not all the time.' Did she even realise how often she tried to blend into the background? 'Sometimes, when you're passionate about a discussion or a new work direction, you forget to take a back seat. Then you're vibrant and persuasive and…*present*.' *He* always noticed her, but he also saw the way she tried not to attract attention. 'But it seems to me you're worried about being seen.'

She said nothing, yet he heard the snatch of indrawn air, saw the sudden lift of her breasts as her breathing turned shallow.

Her vulnerability made his chest clench.

'That's it, isn't it? The reason you wear those cover-up clothes.'

Her eyes narrowed to a gleam of amber fire. 'We can't all afford designer gear.'

'It's not about designer labels, Lily. You've got an attractive body yet you hide it as if you're ashamed. Did you even bring shorts or a sleeveless top here?'

Her silence said she hadn't. His suspicion grew to a certainty as so much became clear. Horror furrowed his gut at the implications.

'No summer clothes, no swimsuit, because you don't want anyone seeing you. You won't go in the water in case you attract attention. Even at dawn when you thought there was no one to see, you wouldn't risk it.' Her silent watchfulness told him he'd hit the truth. 'You want to take cover behind your drab clothes in the hope you won't be noticed.' Raffa was torn between incredulity and pity as he met that stubborn narrowed stare.

'It doesn't work that way, Lily.' His voice grated. He was

staggered at how much he felt for her. 'Don't you realise the more you try to hide, the more obvious you become? The more people watch and wonder? You think they don't see you hiding behind that long hair or those drab clothes? That they don't notice you avoiding them?'

'Who do you think you are to tell me what to wear or how to behave? If I want to wear my hair loose or wear long sleeves, that's my choice.' Her shimmering gaze scraped him from hairline to jaw. 'Even if it displeases a fashion expert like you.'

'And when it stops being a choice? When you deny yourself the pleasure of swimming because you're afraid, not of anything in the water, but of being seen?' Raffa tasted a dull, metallic tang on his tongue. 'That's not choice, Lily. That's when fear has taken over your life.'

The heel of her hand jammed into the centre of his chest, as if she could push him away. Or she needed an outlet for the emotions she'd bottled up so fiercely.

'Don't you *dare* lecture me!' Her voice was a gasp, her breathing too fast, too shallow. 'You have no idea what it's like.'

At the sight of her distress something turned over deep inside. He felt her quiver with the force of her emotions. How long had she dammed it all up? Energy radiated from her in sharp surges that zapped like electricity.

'Then tell me.' He clamped a palm over her hand, holding it to him, feeling the shudders rippling through her. He doubted she noticed.

She shook her head, her hair swirling silk-soft against his hand.

'Tell me, Lily.'

Finally her gaze meshed with his. Those eyes were like amber starbursts now, rimmed with honey-brown. Startling, unique, mesmerising.

'What do you want me to tell you? That for half my life people have looked at me as if I were a freak? They can't help but stare. And they talk to me slowly, in soft voices, as if they're so *sorry* for the way I look they think it's affected my ability to think. Then there are the ones who won't even look at me. They'll have a whole conversation staring at a point over my shoulder to avoid seeing the scar on my face.

'In one day I lost not just my face but my youth, my friend, my fearlessness. The bliss of being *normal*.'

She laughed, the sound off-key, tugging a chord in his belly. 'You have no idea of the jobs I had to give up because of the way people see me. A baker gave me work out of sympathy but lost customers because people didn't want me serving them. Perhaps it made them lose their appetite.'

Raffa tightened his hold, his jaw setting.

'The job in the property office where the other girls couldn't be comfortable working with someone who looked like me. Something about my presence was just too…unsettling.' Sarcasm laced her words and he couldn't blame her.

'But that's not the case now.'

'Sorry?' She looked up at him as if he spoke another language.

'However livid your scar once was, and however stupid some of your old work colleagues. That doesn't apply now.'

She snorted. 'You're going to tell me my scar has suddenly disappeared?'

'I'm telling you that, whatever it looks like, you're a different woman now to the one you were then. You're confident, capable and successful. You can stand up for yourself now. As for the scar—' He lifted his free hand and pushed her hair back behind her ear.

Instantly she stilled, the vibrant energy diminishing to a low-grade hum as if someone had flicked a switch.

Her breath, warm and sweet, feathered his face as he surveyed that taut skin. Raffa tried to imagine how angry it must once have looked, how shocking. But he'd grown so used to it he had trouble seeing it as anything but part of her.

'I've seen far worse,' he said finally.

With an audible snap she shut her mouth, wrenching her hand from his.

'I can't tell you how much better I feel after hearing that!'

Raffa's lips curved at her waspish response. He'd never met anyone so ready to attack in order to defend themselves. It had intrigued him from the first. 'I'm not being patronising, just truthful.'

'And this truth is meant to make my life easier, how?' She tilted her head in mock consideration, her hands going to her hips.

'Let me guess. I'll be so excited that the mighty Raffaele Petri has announced he's seen worse that I'll cut my hair, put on a bikini and spend the rest of my time here chatting up strangers. And, miraculously, no one will notice that one side of my face looks like something out of a horror movie.'

She thrust out her chin, invading his space. 'Get real, Raffaele. Would you touch a woman who looked like this? Of course you wouldn't.'

She opened her mouth for another jibe then shut it when he lifted his palm to the taut skin of her cheek. He heard a hiss and felt her whole body rise with her quick intake of breath. She stared up at him, eyes wide.

He moved his hand over warm skin, exploring, learning the contour of cheekbone and jaw, scar and unblemished skin that was petal-soft. Finally his thumb discovered the rapid tattoo of her pulse. So vital, so fascinating.

Her sweet fruit scent filled his nostrils as he leaned closer, surveying her brilliant eyes, drawn by the inexplicable sense of anticipation trembling between them.

Then, abruptly, she was gone, sliding away from his touch. A few angry strides and she was across the room, shoulders heaving.

He stood where she'd left him, oddly bereft.

What had just happened?

'You have no idea what my life has been like with this scar. Don't you dare tell me it's all okay. I don't need your condescension.'

Raffa was dazed by the emotions she'd evoked. Pity. Protectiveness. Arousal. Anger. And something else.

He'd been trying to help. And what did he get for his pains? That would teach him to try being altruistic!

'Of course, you're the only one in the world whose life has been affected by the way they look.' The words were out before he knew it. 'You need to get over yourself, Lily. That scar can't blight your whole life. Not unless you let it.'

Her gasp was loud in the silence. Once more her hands found her hips and her chin lifted imperiously, like a queen surveying her dominions. Or, given that kindling look, judging some insubordinate slave.

'Get *over* myself?' She shook her head, her stunned eyes never leaving his. 'I don't know what's more insulting. That you pretend I've somehow done this—' she gestured to her face '—to myself. Or that you're looking for sympathy because you've been judged on your looks. Sympathy from *me*?' Her tone said it all.

She was right. Raffa had no grounds to complain. Even if his looks had led him to places, to actions he regretted. He'd have done anything to escape grinding poverty and what he'd done…well, others would say he'd been supremely fortunate. Even if it meant he carried a taint that time couldn't erase.

He'd done what he had to and escaped more lightly than many. As for his looks—he might have been used, and even, some would say, abused, because of them. But he'd made his fortune with his face and emerged triumphant.

Yet in the dark recesses of his soul he acknowledged unexpected kinship with Lily and her problems. Both judged because of the way they appeared.

The difference was that she carried her scars on the outside. His were internal.

'You're absolutely right. I've no cause for complaint. I've got everything a man could want and more.' He didn't add that having everything money could buy didn't counteract the hollowness at the core of a world centred only on himself. The suspicion, too late, that such hollowness would eventually consume him.

'But believe me, Lily, if you don't make a change soon, you won't be able to. Either you let that scar define you or you make the life you want in spite of it.'

Raffa turned on his heel and strode to the door, willing down the tumultuous boil of feelings. He wasn't interested in emotion. He wasn't interested in scars, real or psychological. He was here for a single vital purpose. It was time he got on with it.

He needed to forget the murky... *feelings* Lily evoked and concentrate on Robert Bradshaw. Justice and revenge were much simpler.

CHAPTER SEVEN

NOTHING HELPED. LILY HAD paced her bungalow half the evening, reliving the conversation, coming up with scathing retorts, and still Raffaele's words scraped like a blade scratching flesh. Like the memory of acid on her cheek.

Work hadn't helped. Not that she'd done any work for *him*. She'd dragged out her laptop and spent hours on tasks for her business.

All night she'd worked, but no matter how busy she was, she couldn't stop his words in her brain. Or the fear, deep in her roiling belly, that he might be right. It had stopped her sleeping, despite her exhaustion.

These last years it should have been easier to face the world, especially since surgery had diminished the horror factor of her injury. Yet, perversely, each trip into town had become more difficult than the last. Travelling was a nightmare of self-consciousness, and forcing herself into that New York office every day...

Lily shook her head, hair sliding reassuringly across her cheeks. She'd had to face down panic attacks just to get through the door.

You think they don't see you hiding behind that long hair or those drab clothes?

She stilled. He'd all but accused her of being a coward. She who'd weathered such pain, such grief, and then had to face the unmistakable, if unspoken, blame of the whole community when *she'd* been the one to survive rather than Rachel. Vibrant, pretty, life-of-the-party Rachel, star of the swim squad, the debating team, academically gifted, on her way to stellar success in whatever field she chose.

Rachel, her best friend.

Lily gulped down a sob that shook her from her shoulders to her soles.

She didn't do self-pity. She didn't!

She'd faced medical treatments and long convalescence stoically when all her peers were enjoying themselves. Hadn't she forced herself to succeed, refusing to give up when one job after another failed? She'd been determined to stand on her own feet, not be a burden to her worried parents and protective brothers. She'd worked like a slave to establish her own business, carve success and security.

Security away from the world.

A continent away from her family and the last of her friends.

The air rushed from her chest as if she'd been stabbed in the lungs. She felt herself deflating, crumpling, her knees collapsing till she sagged onto the edge of the bed.

It hurt to breathe. Blackness clouded the edge of her vision like churning storm clouds. Spots of white burst around her as the world turned grey, then darker. Her head swam. Any second now the blackness would consume her.

Then, with a huge, juddering heave, her lungs opened up, drawing in air that seared all the way down her aching throat. The grey retreated. The room, with its pale furnishings and bright tropical accents, came into focus. Through the window she saw the golden bloom of dawn fringe the horizon, spreading across the water towards her.

Raffaele was right.

She was scared. More than scared—she was petrified.

When had it happened?

She'd been so busy forcing herself to face the world, the need to find a job, build a career and be independent from her worried, loving parents. She hadn't noticed when wariness had gradually become withdrawal, independence had turned to isolation and the comfort of her own home had become a cage.

Reluctantly, each muscle protesting, she turned her head.

Across the bed lay strewn the items she'd tossed there last evening when her rage had been white-hot. A staff member from the resort boutique had brought them in glossy, silver-ribboned bags. Only one person could have sent them.

A broad-brimmed hat, a bright skirt of some soft fabric that slipped through her fingers like cool water. A sleeveless top sporting a designer label, a one-piece swimsuit and a long, loose gauzy cover-up, for wearing while lolling by the pool. There was even a pair of cute sandals with ribbons that tied around the ankles.

Each in her size.

Each worth more than she'd spend on clothes in a year.

Each mocking her.

Her fury had spiked at the idea of Raffaele ordering them, daring her to wear them.

As if it was any of his business what she wore.

Now they lay, taunting her, a challenge she couldn't ignore.

How had he known what she hadn't recognised in herself? It wasn't as if she were important to him, yet he'd taken time to see her as more than an employee. He'd seen her as an individual. As someone who counted. He'd forced her to understand herself clearly for the first time in years.

The pain of that self-knowledge tore at her.

Gritting her teeth, Lily reached out and touched the swimsuit. The fabric was soft, fluid and silky, frighteningly thin.

It gave nowhere to hide.

Raffa flicked water from his eyes, treading water. Five laps of the bay and his chest was on fire, his legs and arms like jelly. But exertion hadn't brought relief.

All night he'd been haunted by Lily's face when he'd told her to move on with her life, stop taking cover and ignore her scar.

His gut clenched, making him sink below the surface

till he kicked harder. Who was he to tell her how to live? How could he begin to imagine what it was like to be her?

Sometimes his arrogance appalled even himself.

He turned from the headland, back towards the bay, ready for another punishing lap, when a lone figure on the beach stopped him. A figure with pale limbs, long hair and a body clad in bronze. Dawn light caught each supple angle and sweet curve. It burnished the taut swimsuit that clung to Lily's delectable body.

Why had he ever thought it a good idea for her to bare herself?

Testosterone surged, weighting his body, tightening each muscle, turning his lungs into a furnace where each breath was an ache of pure heat.

She was unadorned. He tried to tell himself it was the simplicity of the picture she made that affected him. But he'd seen countless women—clothed, unclothed, in ball gowns and swimsuits, towels and wisps of nothing. None affected him like this.

He took in her ravaged cheek, lit by the morning sun as she shook her hair off her face. The movement was one of impatience, determination, and it made his heart jump.

His lips curved in a proud smile. He hadn't been sure she'd accept the gauntlet he'd thrown down. She could just as easily have nestled further into that protective shell, cutting herself off from the world. From him.

He admired her fierce determination. She was a worthy adversary.

Raffa reminded himself she wasn't an adversary, but an employee.

Except in the oldest contest of all, the struggle between male and female.

He couldn't ignore it any longer. For almost two months he'd pretended Lily Nolan was intriguing because of her prickly ways and quick mind. And her determination not to be cowed by his wealth or position. They were part of it, but not all. Denial only went so far, especially in a man who, after years of celibacy, of utter disinterest in sex, felt the sudden rush and roar of desire.

She waded out till the water was hip deep, her smile widening with each step. The glow on her face made him feel like a voyeur, watching an intensely private moment, yet he couldn't look away. He'd never seen her like this, so strong and free and elemental.

In a sinuous movement she lifted her hands over her head and dived. Raffa waited till he saw her begin a strong, easy stroke. Then he dragged in a rough breath and turned to the headland. He'd have to clamber over the rocks instead of sand to get out but she deserved her solitude.

Lily shivered as the warm sea breeze feathered her face, her bare neck and legs. Despite the blaze of sunshine she was chilled to the marrow, frozen by apprehension. She'd never felt more vulnerable since that first day out of hospital.

She'd chosen this chair by the poolside out of bravado, proving to herself she wasn't the coward Raffaele thought her.

But it seemed she was. Her joints felt as if they'd been welded solid with the effort it took to remain here, in full public view, and wearing so little.

'Can I join you?' The voice, like rich caramel, swirled around Lily. Beckoning warmth encircled her, coaxing taut muscles to ease just a little.

Something like relief fizzed in her veins.

He'd come.

She hadn't expected him to.

Or wanted him, she assured herself.

Slowly Lily turned. Raffaele Petri stood on the flagstones, his back to the pool and the outdoor café/bar where guests gathered. Against the azure of the pool his gold-toned body, bare but for damp board shorts and a half-buttoned shirt, glowed. The sun gilded his tousled hair, but it was his eyes, deep-set and probing, that snagged her attention.

A flare of heat ran through her veins then dropped to eddy in her stomach.

She should be furious with him.

She *wanted* to be furious.

But she was grateful too. He'd ripped the blinkers from her eyes.

She shrugged, stiff muscles protesting. 'Sounds good. With you here they'll forget to look at me.'

More likely the other resort guests would wonder what the most beautiful man on the planet was doing with such an ugly woman. Beauty and the Beast.

She reminded herself she didn't care. That was her mantra as of dawn this morning. She'd given up worrying about the effect she had on others. Or she would, she assured herself, once she got used to being out in public. For now she'd pretend to ignore the prickle across her skin as the weight of so many curious eyes grazed her.

'They're too busy worrying about their suntans to pay attention to us.'

Lily stifled a snort of disbelief. No one could help but notice Raffaele. He hooked a chair close and sank into it, the fluid grace of his athletic body mesmerising.

Yet he wasn't at ease. The smile edging his lips wasn't his usual confident one. It looked lopsided, almost self-conscious.

The idea confused her. She snatched at it greedily, anything to distract herself from her surroundings.

Raffaele was utterly sure of himself. He was powerful, able to get what he wanted with the click of his fingers. Nor did a crisis faze him. She'd seen him work through unexpected and potentially calamitous developments in the office. He'd been unflappable, thriving on challenge.

'Espresso.' He nodded to the waiter who'd materialised

beside them. 'And…?' He looked questioningly at her empty glass.

'Another fruit juice, thank you, Charles.' She lifted her head to meet the waiter's eyes, feeling the sun warm her bare cheeks. In a fit of defiant energy she'd coiled her hair up, using every pin she possessed to secure it. No more covering her cheeks. No more concealment. It had sounded simple back in her bungalow, but here, where everyone passing could see her, she felt exposed.

'You're on first-name terms with the waiter?'

'You disapprove?' She closed her eyes, telling herself she enjoyed the feel of the sun on her face.

'Not at all. But a lot of people don't bother to discover the names of people who serve them.'

'I'm a researcher, remember. You'd be amazed how much I've found out from talking with the locals. But the fact is they're so friendly I enjoy getting to know them.' They'd made her feel welcome despite her nerves in a new place, meeting new people.

'Lily?'

She opened her eyes to find Raffaele leaning close. The blaze of those ocean-bright eyes did odd things to her breathing.

'Yes?'

He paused and she frowned, wondering at his unaccustomed hesitation.

'I apologise.'

Lily stared, watching his lips form the words but not believing the evidence of her eyes or her ears.

'Apologise?' Raffaele Petri? He might not be the ogre who'd once threatened to destroy her business. He might even be kind. But she'd never heard him admit regret.

The line of his mouth kinked in a brittle smile. 'Last night. What I said to you—'

'Don't.' She shook her head, again hyper-aware of the

warmth of the sun on her cheeks instead of the swish of her hair.

'You were right.' The words were thick in her throat, an admission of her own blindness. She should have seen the truth sooner. 'I *was* hiding.' It was the hardest admission she'd ever made.

He nodded, his gaze fixed on her face. A tremor ran through her, her fingers twitching with the almost unstoppable urge to wrench her hair down and conceal herself.

'I know. I wasn't apologising for that. But for the way I spoke to you. I'm sorry. I was angry, arrogant. I should have been more tactful.'

Lily's mouth sagged. No apology for what he'd done, just the way he'd done it. What must it be like to be so utterly sure of yourself?

But he wasn't. She read his wariness and regret. She'd swear that was doubt in his set features. The realisation tipped the world out of balance for the second time in less than twenty-four hours.

'What are you smiling about?' His brow furrowed.

'Nothing. Really.' She paused and dragged in a fortifying breath, watching the waiter place their drinks on the table then leave. 'I... Thank you. I think if you'd been kind I wouldn't have listened. You *made* me listen because you didn't mince your words.'

She owed him so much. Without pausing for second thoughts she reached out and touched him lightly on the back of the hand.

Instantly energy fizzed and crackled up her arm, prickling her skin and drawing the hairs on her nape upright.

Dismay wrenched at her insides. She had an immediate, overwhelming certainty that she'd gone too far. Not because he looked disapproving, but because of the dart and fizz of pleasure making her body come alive in a whole new way. She looked down, *willing* her fingers not to close around his. It took far too long for her hand to obey her brain, yanking back as if scalded.

Her eyes fluttered shut as she sucked in a horrified breath. How could such a little thing be so devastating?

'Lily?' That low voice hummed through every erogenous zone in her body. She had to get a grip. She was twenty-eight, not some teenager.

Except when it came to dealing with attractive men that was exactly how she felt: fourteen and flustered, gauche and totally inexperienced.

Lily snapped open her eyes, forcing herself to meet that stunning blue stare. 'I accept your apology. I hated the way you said it but I'm glad you did.' Her pent-up breath expelled in a whoosh. 'I can't believe I never saw it before.'

'Hey, don't beat yourself up. You're a remarkable woman. You've achieved so much. And, no, I don't just mean your work for me.' He gestured to her cheek. 'Coping with that would tax anyone. You've done superbly.'

'Why are you being so kind?'

'Kind?' His eyes rounded. 'I'm realistic. What you've built for yourself, the woman you are—that took guts and determination.'

He meant it. This wasn't like the well-meaning bonhomie of her family, whose exuberant praise for even the smallest achievements made her feel...not patronised... but as if perhaps those small achievements were the best she could ever do.

Guilt smote her. It wasn't like that, really. Her family had been on her side through the darkest days. She wouldn't have got through what she had without them. Of course they'd wanted to celebrate each small step forward. But eventually she'd become claustrophobic, encircled by their protectiveness.

Yet Raffaele's no-nonsense approach, his confrontational attitude, challenging her to rise above her fear, had made all the difference.

She cleared her throat. 'I could say the same about you. You've come a long way.'

Was it imagination or did the shutters come down on his expression? Strange. She'd never considered he had no-go territory. Raffaele seemed so confident and at ease.

A moment later the impression was gone. He lifted his coffee cup for a leisurely sip, leaning into his chair, one arm looped over the back. The pose stretched the gap of his half-open shirt, revealing a sprinkling of hair across his tightly muscled chest.

Lily blinked, cursing her inability to concentrate. This was the closest she'd ever been to a virile, attractive man in his prime and it tied her brain in knots.

A woman on the far side of the pool stumbled to a stop, staring, before recovering her poise and her dropped beach towel. The fact Lily wasn't the only one responding to Raffaele's stunning looks didn't make her feel better.

It made her feel...possessive. He was here with *her*, even if it was just their business connection and his concern for her welfare that linked them.

'That was another life.' His smile was brief but dazzling, yet Lily couldn't help feeling he used it to distract her.

He didn't want to talk about his past? She could relate to that. She opened her mouth to ask about his plans for this resort, if and when he acquired it from Robert Bradshaw, but he got in first.

'You'll need to be careful of the sun.' He gestured to the filmy caftan of bronze and golden brown she wore over her swimsuit. 'Delightful as that outfit is, there's no sun protection and your skin is like cream.'

Was that a compliment or an accusation? A reminder that she'd lived the last few years immured at home, using work as an excuse not to go out?

To Lily's amazement she felt heat creep under her skin. A heat that had nothing to do with the sunshine and everything to do with Raffaele Petri's heavy-lidded gaze on her body. It had been more than a decade since she'd blushed but that stare was unlike anything she'd ever experienced. Men didn't look at her that way. Ever.

'Where's the hat I ordered for you? You should at least be wearing that.'

It was a sign of her stress that she'd actually forgotten the clothes she wore had been bought by him.

Suddenly the slinky bronze swimsuit felt too clingy. And as for the gossamer-thin cover-up—its light-as-air delicacy against her arms and bare thighs now made her imagine another touch...the touch of trailing masculine fingers.

'I don't need a nanny, Raffaele.' She might have problems going out among people but she was twenty-eight, able to watch out for sunburn.

'Just as well.' His drawl rang alarm bells in some never-before-accessed part of her brain. 'Because I don't feel at all like a nanny.'

His expression jammed the breath in her lungs. Worse, it drew the heat that skimmed her body down into a spiralling vortex.

Lily clamped her hands on the arms of her chair, willing herself not to shift restlessly. But his look was making her feel...aroused. Aware. Awash with longing.

Her nipples tightened into buds and she crossed her arms, hoping she looked annoyed, anything but needy.

It would be excruciatingly awful if he realised how attracted she was. Enough to imagine she read sexual interest in his glance.

'That's another thing. I owe you for the clothes. I know you only sent them as a challenge, to dare me out of my comfort zone, but I have to pay you back.'

Once more his gaze skimmed over her, with the swift precision of a connoisseur. What did he see, apart from her blemished face? A too-pale body that held no allure when compared with the women he knew? Of course that was it. He'd even bought this outfit in shades of brown, surely a sign he saw her as a drab sparrow.

'And for the pleasure of seeing you in them.'

'Sorry?' The screech of her chair scraping back on the flagstones almost obliterated the sound of her shock-diminished voice. Her heart thrummed so hard against her ribs she felt light-headed.

'I said, I wanted to see you in them. You've got a lovely body, Lily. You should be proud of it.'

She shook her head.

'You've made your point about me being a recluse. You don't need to say things that aren't true.' He had no idea how cruel that was. How badly a woman who'd never had such a compliment in her life yearned for it to be real.

She'd spent half a lifetime being told that true beauty was on the inside. But some pathetic, juvenile part of her still longed to be thought pretty. Just once.

'You think I'm lying?' His dark eyebrows steepled together. 'You know me, Lily. I always get straight to the point. These days I tell the unvarnished truth instead of any easy lies.'

He leaned forward, closing the gap between them. His bluer than blue eyes pinioned her. 'You have a beautiful body, Lily, and I enjoy looking at you. *That's* the truth.'

CHAPTER EIGHT

RAFFA WATCHED HER stalk from the pool terrace, along the path through the gardens. Head up, shoulders back, long legs supple and strong, hips swaying in unconscious invitation. She was as alluring as any classically beautiful model he'd known.

More. There was nothing artificial about Lily. From those pert breasts to that searing golden-brown stare she was authentic.

Desirable.

Around the poolside heads turned to follow her progress. Raffa saw women lean close together, whispering, their expressions varying from sympathy to horror.

No doubt about it, Lily had been brave sitting here alone, without even a hat to conceal her scarred face.

But for every female shudder he caught more masculine stares. Some overt, some discreet, all fixed on the delectable sway of her body.

Raffa tried to analyse what it was about her that fired his libido. The swell of her hips? The ripe thrust of her breasts? The long, seductive curve of thigh and calf?

Maybe the way her voice turned to a throaty purr when she was annoyed. Or the curious mix of vulnerability and vivacity that kept him on his toes. Even her prickly defensiveness appealed, provoking him time and again to pursue the woman who tried to disguise herself.

For the first time he was attracted to a woman's mind, her thoughts and character, as well as her body.

Whatever this was, he'd passed the point of hoping it would go away. She'd stirred him out of sexual apathy so profoundly he felt wired, attuned to her as a predator to his prey. Her every shift of mood jangled his senses, under-mining his concentration on the vital deal he'd come here to close. He should be focused on Bradshaw, yet Lily was a distraction he couldn't ignore.

Worryingly, she also aroused dormant feelings—con-cern, protectiveness, caring. Feelings expunged the day his childhood ended. The day Gabriella had been found dead.

Raffa sank back in his seat, winded by the devastating simplicity of what he faced.

For the first time in his life there was no careful con-sideration of pros and cons, of benefits versus risks. Just untrammelled desire, simple and unprecedented.

That explained his less than impressive performance just now. No one hearing him would believe he'd once made a living out of sweet-talking women. He'd known how to pan-der to female fantasies, to become whatever they wanted for long enough to get what he in turn needed from them. He'd been smooth but never obvious. He'd made each one feel special. That had been his gift and his greatest asset.

The question was, had he completely lost his touch?

Raffa was lost in thought when a flash of colour caught his eye. A stream of dark gold as familiar as the reflection he saw in the mirror if ever he bothered to look. Colour as rich as ancient coins, hoarded for a king's pleasure, but instead of cold metal this was a ribbon burnished by the sun, cascading down a woman's back. It rippled in soft waves as she moved.

Emotion clutched his chest, digging talons deep into his heart, squeezing his lungs. His breath stopped on a harsh rasp. She moved again, slender arms pushing her hair over her shoulder in a gesture he'd known from infancy.

Gabriella.

Raffa opened his mouth till instinct, more primitive than logic, stopped him. To call out would break the magic.

He wanted to run to her. Pour out his apologies for not

behaving better, for not appreciating how lucky he was to
have her. For driving her away in frustration that last night.
He was twelve again and desperate. He felt grief and regret, shame and hope.

Till she moved again and the magic was lost.

It wasn't Gabriella.

Of course it wasn't. Gabriella was twenty-one years'
dead. Yet for a moment she'd been vividly alive again.
Raffa's heart sprinted in a sickening, uneven gallop, his
lungs atrophied and he forced his fisted hands to loosen.

The young woman moved again, walking through the
shallow end of the pool, and her walk wasn't Gabriella's.
Her hair wasn't down to her waist and she was boyishly
slim whereas Gabriella had been curvy.

One thing they had in common though. They were both
in their teens. The girl was around fifteen or sixteen, much
younger than the man helping her from the pool.

Raffa was turning away when his gaze sharpened. That
wasn't her father taking her arm. He recognised the fleshy
face and ham-like hands. Hands that lingered on her hips.

Robert Bradshaw. The man he'd avoided since arriv-
ing. He had no interest in seeing him till he was ready to
make his move. Making Bradshaw sweat, waiting for that
moment, was a bonus.

But it wasn't the deal on Raffa's mind now. It was Gabriella and how Bradshaw had ushered her aboard his boat
twenty-one years ago, an arm hovering near her waist as
he offered champagne.

The next morning Gabriella was dead.

There was a crash and Raffa looked down to see glass
splintered across the paving where he'd knocked his drink.

Bradshaw heard it too, his head snapping up. Seconds
later he was patting the girl and murmuring in her ear before leaving her.

'Signor Petri. It's good to see you at last.' He lunged forward to shake hands but Raffa avoided the gesture, leaning down to collect broken glass.

'Leave that. It's what the staff are for.' The Englishman turned as a waiter hurried out with a brush and pan. 'About time! You should have been here instantly.'

'It's fine.' Raffa nodded to the waiter. 'My fault.'

Seconds later the glass was cleared and Bradshaw hefted himself into a chair. 'I've been wanting to catch up with you. We've a lot to discuss.' He waved expansively. 'Excellent idea to come here personally to see the resort before we close a deal. It's really something, isn't it?'

Behind his air of ease Raffa detected strain. Good. That was a start. Ideally Raffa would see him behind bars for the rest of his life but, as that wasn't possible, the revenge he'd planned would have to be enough.

'It's peaceful.' He saw Bradshaw frown, dismayed at Raffa's lack of praise. The man was no negotiator, letting his fear show.

'Come to my house and I'll see you get some action.' Bradshaw leaned in. 'Come to dinner. I'll throw a private party. I'm sure you'll enjoy it.'

Raffa was shaking his head before Bradshaw stopped speaking. 'I'm afraid not.' He didn't bother giving an excuse. Let him stew.

Bradshaw's smile grew guarded. 'Later in the week then. Let me know when you're free to discuss business. In the meantime, relax, enjoy.' He leaned close enough for Raffa to smell sweat and expensive aftershave.

'Would you like some female company to amuse you while you're here? It would be very discreet.' When Raffa didn't respond he continued, flicking a glance across the pool. 'A nice, fresh girl. Blonde, maybe? Or redhead? Just say the word.'

Nausea clutched Raffa's belly as he followed Bradshaw's leering gaze to the girl he'd seen earlier. His hands dug so tight into his chair's armrests he'd probably mark the metal like he wanted to mark Bradshaw's face. It was a miracle he held back, a miracle possible only because he knew Bradshaw would pay with everything he had and everything he'd ever wanted, once this deal went through.

'No,' Raffa croaked. 'Nothing. I'm here for peace and quiet.'

Abruptly he levered himself up, barely acknowledging the other man's babble about meeting soon for sundowners at his house.

Raffa nodded and strode away. He told himself his tactic to make Bradshaw sweat could only help negotiations. But the truth was he couldn't stomach being within spitting distance of the man. He didn't trust himself not to do him violence.

CHAPTER NINE

SEEING BRADSHAW LEFT a sour taste in Raffa's mouth. He wanted this wrapped up. But after more long distance discussions with his legal team, he acknowledged there were still matters to be sorted before he brought Bradshaw to his knees. The delay rankled, but at least it had the bonus of making Bradshaw even more desperate.

When Lily knocked on his villa door for their early evening meeting, relief hit like the smack of an ocean wave. Raffa needed distraction from his circling thoughts but more, he'd wondered if she'd show after what had passed between them.

He couldn't explain it but since seeing Bradshaw and that girl at the pool, Raffa had been unsettled, ridiculously on edge as emotions crowded close. Calm evaded him as if the thick skin he'd spent a lifetime nurturing had been scraped raw. He felt… He *felt*! And it wasn't just hatred of Bradshaw.

He told himself he needed the distraction of work.

Yet Lily looked anything but professional in the clothes he'd chosen. An aqua scoop-necked top and wraparound skirt in aqua with a swirl of gold that fluttered enticingly around her legs. She hesitated in the doorway, giving him time to drink her in and to stifle the urge to haul her close. His gaze dipped briefly, taking in the ankle ties on the sandals that accentuated her sexy calves.

An appreciative smile curled inside him, a smile he repressed. She was skittish enough already. 'You're here. Good. We've a lot to get through.'

Predictably, instead of stiffening at his tone, Lily seemed

reassured as she stepped over the threshold and onto the polished wood floor.

'This is for you.' She offered an envelope.

Her resignation? The idea tore his thoughts completely free of Bradshaw and business. His chest hollowed as he made himself reach for it, noting the way she relinquished it as soon as he grasped it.

Had he pushed her too far? She was like a porcupine, raising spiky quills if he got too near. Yet he knew she wanted him as much as he wanted her. If only he could entice her to let down her guard.

Mouth firm, Raffa tore open the envelope. 'Money?'

'For the clothes.' Her voice was as tight as her shoulders.

Briefly Raffa considered admitting it had been pure pleasure choosing clothes for her, ones that suited her and made the most of her delectable body. That if he'd had his way he wouldn't have stopped there. He'd have bought the ivory lace nightgown for starters. Just for the pleasure of seeing her in it, then peeling it away.

'Consider it a business perk.' He held the envelope out to her. 'I insisted on bringing you here.'

She shook her head. For once there was no accompanying ripple of brown silk around her shoulders. She'd pinned her hair up again. Pinned it so tight it was a wonder she didn't have a headache.

Definitely one for gestures, his *piccola istrice*. How sharp, he wondered, were her quills?

'I buy my own clothes.'

'Even if you didn't choose them?' If she'd had her way there'd have been more concealing shirts and baggy trousers.

'I accepted them, therefore I pay.' As she said it her hand rose to her neckline. A sign of nerves?

It struck him anew how difficult it must be for Lily to reveal herself like this. But he knew better than to show his thoughts, much less praise her courage.

'Fine.' He tossed the envelope onto the table where he'd drawn up two chairs. 'Now, let's get started. I want to go over every last detail. Nothing can be missed.'

As ever when they worked, time slid by unnoticed. Lily began to relax as Raffaele focused on business.

There were no kindling glances or personal comments. They were again boss and employee, or more precisely, colleagues. Raffaele recognised the expertise of his team and treated them with respect. Lily thrived on feeling appreciated.

'When are you meeting Robert Bradshaw?' They'd been at the resort two nights and she knew there'd been at least one invitation to dine at Bradshaw's house on the far side of the island.

'In good time.' Raffa's voice was brusque.

'But isn't that why you're here?' Raffaele had driven his team like the devil to prepare for this deal. He'd come here himself rather than delegate. 'You're deliberately delaying?'

One eyebrow rose. 'The time's not right. I'm waiting till he's heard confirmation his play for more capital has failed. Then he'll be more amenable to my terms.'

'What if it doesn't fail?'

'Oh, it will.' Raffa's eyes flashed with an expression that unsettled, until Lily reminded herself they were discussing Robert Bradshaw.

She had no sympathy for the Englishman. Born with wealth, he'd squandered his fortune through excess. His few attempts at running any of the businesses he'd inherited had ended disastrously and now he teetered on the brink of ruin. Not that you'd know it from his lavish lifestyle.

'You're turning the screw?'

Raffa leaned back, linking his hands behind his head. The movement emphasised the heavy breadth of muscled shoulders and taut biceps beneath his casual shirt. Lily dragged her gaze to the old deeds she'd unearthed. But her breath came in shallow little bursts. She didn't feel professional but dizzy and shamefully entranced.

How much longer could she pretend disinterest?

'I've shown my hand by coming here. That's enough. No point letting Bradshaw think he'll get everything he wants.' Venom dripped from Raffaele's tone as he said the Englishman's name, confirming her suspicion of bad blood between the men. Yet her searches had uncovered no link.

'He's desperate for a partner to put up cash to renovate the place. Even he recognises profits aren't what they could be and it's his last money-making asset.'

'So the longer he waits, the more desperate he becomes.'

'Unless he finds another partner. It's a calculated risk not to rush in. The resort is an appealing investment.'

Lily nodded. It was like Paradise. She wouldn't be surprised if at least one of the other companies she'd worked for, De Laurentis Enterprises, was interested.

'But he wants you because you've got the golden touch.' Raffaele's hotels were a byword for discreet luxury that appealed to the seriously wealthy who sought respite from the paparazzi. And who had deep, deep pockets.

'It seems a shame to change the place. It's wonderful as it is.' Her gaze drifted to the white curve of beach framed by lush gardens. To her surprise the bright sky had darkened to indigo, torches lighting the path through the trees. It was later than she'd thought.

'It needs updating to attract the clientele Bradshaw wants.'

'The way the poolside bar has been updated?' Lily pursed her lips. While the rest of the resort had a graceful if slightly worn charm with plantation shutters, airy rooms and individual bungalows, the bar was sleek, black-tiled and ostentatiously modern with vivid neon light displays and uncomfortable, trendy metal chairs.

Raffaele's lip curled. 'Bradshaw's one effort at updating the place. The man's got no sense. The clientele he wants to attract can fly to New York or elsewhere if they want urban modern. They'll come here for premium luxury and privacy. And to experience the Caribbean, its tastes and laid-back style.'

'So what would you do? How would you change it?'

'Reduce the number of bungalows for a start.' He responded almost before she'd finished speaking. 'Keep the best and get rid of the rest. People pay for the privilege of privacy. Remodel and upgrade everything. Each villa would have its own pool, spa, butler and chef. Put in a truly fabulous restaurant on the hill featuring a new twist on traditional local flavours and produce. Bring in the absolute best in everything. Improve...'

'What?' She leaned across the table.

Abruptly Raffaele shook his head. 'It doesn't matter. All that matters is getting Bradshaw to accept my offer.' His voice was harsh, his words clipped.

Lily sat back. It was stupid to feel rebuffed. She wouldn't be involved when Raffaele put his plans into action. He had other staff for that. But she'd been caught up in his enthusiasm. His energy had drawn her, making her want more.

There was no more. Not with Raffaele. Not unless it was legwork for some other project.

She swallowed, realising it wasn't even his vision for the resort that had held her spellbound. It was Raffaele. She'd never known a man so charismatic, so vital. If she reached out a hand towards him she knew she'd feel the buzz and zap of energy radiating from him.

Yet the desire to touch was more than that.

She wanted to touch him the way a woman touched her lover.

Lily stood. 'It's time I left.'

He stood when she did, his expression unreadable. 'There's no rush. I've ordered dinner to be served here.'

Dinner? With Raffaele?

Lily felt the punch of her heart against her ribs. She

imagined them sitting, drinking in the view, sipping wine and feasting on seafood as they relaxed in each other's company. He'd be charming and she'd be witty and insightful and when their gazes locked she'd read heat and hunger and—

'We've finished for the day, haven't we?' Her voice was scratchy. Better that than needy, she told herself. Heat crept up her throat at the thoughts she'd harboured. 'Unless there's something else you wanted me to do.' She made a production of gathering her gear.

'There is, as it happens.'

Her head snapped up as those deep cadences wrapped around her. 'Yes?'

'I want you to dine with me.'

Lily blinked. 'Why?'

'I want your company.'

Her fingers curled around her laptop. She felt out of her depth.

The look he gave her, grave yet knowing, sent a wobble from her chest all the way to her knees. It was the sort of look she'd imagined a man gave a woman he was interested in. It made her pulse flutter in her throat as if she'd swallowed a swarm of bright island butterflies.

Lily had never received such a look before.

She didn't know what to do with it.

Or with the hammering excitement within.

She swallowed hard. Clearly she was superimposing her secret cravings on him. Raffaele Petri had a host of beautiful women to choose from. It was laughable to think he could be attracted to her.

Beyond laughable. It was pathetic.

'It's time I went.' Before she made a fool of herself.

'You said that before.' He crossed his arms over his chest and it struck her for the first time that he stood between her and the door.

Lily spread clammy hands on the table, hoping its solidity would help penetrate the fog in her brain. Help her think straight and stop imagining things.

Except, when she looked up, Raffaele's blue eyes sparked with something that made her belly curl and her nipples bud against her bra. Her skin felt tight, as if the woman inside were bursting to escape.

'It's true. We've finished for the night.'

Slowly he shook his head, the movement accentuating the shadows beneath his high cheekbones.

'I sincerely hope not.' Was it imagination or was his voice thicker, his accent more pronounced? It ran through her veins like warm caramel.

Lily dragged her hands from the table as if its surface was electrified. A large hand snapped out and captured her wrist. Instantly she stilled, all except for the quiver reverberating from her tingling fingers up her arm and down to the soles of her feet.

'What do you want, Raffaele? What are you playing at?' Old habit came to the rescue and her chin jutted. She'd spent half a lifetime pretending to be impervious to hurt.

'What do you think I want?' It was the voice of her dreams, seductive, alluring and full of desire.

Impossible!

She yanked her hand free, stepping out of reach. Her breath sawed through searing lungs.

He was flirting. Sending her that half-lidded look that had turned a single photo into a multi-million-dollar success for a famous men's clothing company.

The impact of it in the flesh, on *her* flesh, was devastating.

'Stop it, Raffaele!' She was almost beyond caring that he might hear the hurt beneath her belligerence. She needed to get away. 'I don't...' She shook her head, wishing she hadn't made a point of pinning her hair up, wishing it could swish around her face, concealing an expression she feared must reveal the yearning in her soul.

'Don't what?'

Don't flirt. She didn't know how. Had no experience of it. Which made this game he played even more cruel.

'What are you afraid of, Lily?' His voice, rough suede, caressed her skin, drawing it to tingling life.

You.

Of you and everything you make me feel.

'I didn't think anything fazed you, Lily. You're so feisty, so focused.'

She cleared her throat to speak as he moved close enough for her to inhale the tantalising scent of warm male skin, salt spice and the sea. But determination wasn't enough. Not when she looked up into ocean-blue eyes. They burned with a heat that beckoned to every feminine instinct she'd spent fourteen years suppressing.

'Is it this you're afraid of?' His head lowered and warmth brushed her lips. The soft caress of perfectly sculpted lips. The fleeting, beckoning taste of Paradise as his tongue slicked the seam of her mouth.

Lily's eyelids flickered, weighted by the desire rolling through her, inexorably growing, expanding, clogging every sense. All she knew was the scent and taste of Raffaele, the heat of his breath on her lips, the pulse of longing throbbing within.

Air brushed her mouth as his lips left hers and for a heartbeat nothing moved. She didn't even breathe.

Lily forced her eyes open. Azure depths captured her and it was as if she'd ventured too far out to sea. Except she wasn't sinking, she was floating, buoyed by an anticipation so acute she felt she'd shatter if he didn't put an end to it and kiss her properly.

'I'm not afraid,' she lied.

She was terrified. Thrilled. Exultant. Curious.

Lily felt her hand settle against the muscled plane of his chest. Beneath her palm beat a steady pulse that seemed leisurely compared with her own wildly careering heartbeat.

He was *real*. Not the phantom lover of her dreams. His flesh was hotter than hers even through his shirt.

His chest rose under her touch, making her aware of the masculine power beneath the designer panache. The air of languid relaxation Raffaele so often adopted was a front, she realised, as sparks tickled her palm, racing up her arm. The man was all potent power.

But he was her boss. He was one of the most beautiful men on the planet, and she—

'Lily.' His voice was so deep she felt its reverberation in her belly. His hand was hard as it clamped her palm to his chest.

She shifted back. 'This is a mistake.'

He moved with her, his thigh brushing hers. Ripples coursed up her leg to the spot between her thighs where a different pulse beat— needy and quick.

'No mistake. Admit it, Lily. This feels *right*.'

His left hand captured her nape, long fingers spearing through her hair to hold her still as his head slanted down.

Time moved in infinitely slow seconds. Slow enough for her to realise that, despite his hold, she had only to turn her head or step back and she'd be free.

But she didn't move. It *did* feel right. More, it felt inevitable. Why pretend when for weeks she'd wondered what it would be like to kiss Raffaele?

His lips touched hers again, once, twice, before settling on her mouth, sealing her breath with his. For a moment he held utterly still. She absorbed the rich, warm scent of his skin, the delicious tang of him on her tongue, the long body hard up against hers, and the gentleness of his hand at the back of her head, cradling, tender...

Then those azure eyes closed, his head tilting as he delved between her parted lips. One swiping caress and sensation shuddered down her backbone and further, weakening her knees. They trembled as she clutched him, drawn by the slide of his mouth, his probing tongue and the waves of need, dark and intoxicating, that buffeted her.

His hand tightened on her skull, the angle of his mouth changed and the kiss grew harder, insistent, demanding. Raffaele drew her tongue between his lips, sucking, and a shot of adrenaline, of *something,* fired in her blood. The pulse between her legs quickened, her nipples against his chest so sensitive she almost cried out as each muffled breath abraded them against him. She was on fire, burning up in a heat he both kindled and promised to assuage.

Was it possible to climax just from kissing?

Lily slipped her hands up to clasp his face, framing hard bone and taut skin, learning sculpted contours as his tongue flicked hers, inviting her to join him, to give in.

A mighty shudder ran through her, a sigh that made no sound in the whirling ecstasy of the moment. A sigh of surrender as Lily let herself go and for the first time in her life kissed a man.

He'd guessed she'd be delicious. He'd expected fire beneath her guarded prickliness.

But still he wasn't prepared. Lily's slender body turned to flame against him, all eager passion and flagrant, hungry need. He felt her shake in his hold, her whole body trembling. But not with fear. Not when she kissed him back with such glorious abandon.

He couldn't get enough, clutching her greedily.

Tongue on tongue, lips against lips, heart to heart, soft belly to quickening arousal—she was all he'd hoped for and more. The scent of sweet pears vied with a tantalising hint of musk and she tasted…he couldn't describe her flavour, other than addictive.

Raffa drew her against his mouth and his groin. How long since he'd felt that urgent spiral of desire? That restless hunger to possess?

For years he'd been celibate, uninterested in women. Yet

Lily, with her shaking hands and clumsy kisses, turned him on more than any practised seductress.

She pressed in, her teeth mashing his lip. Her untutored eagerness was beguiling as nothing he'd ever experienced. Raffaele was used to women blasé about sex, who enjoyed it but were never surprised by it.

By contrast he sensed shock as well as delight in Lily's response. As if all this was new.

Would you touch a woman who looked like this?
Of course you wouldn't.

Her words slammed into him. And the memory of Lily's grave eyes as she'd said it, hurt dragging her mouth down.

In the midst of the maelstrom something inside him stilled, held its breath.

Instinct urged him to take advantage of her eagerness. But some damned part of his brain had begun working, sifting what she'd said, analysing the inexperience in her kisses and clutching hands.

It couldn't be.

No woman got to twenty-eight without being kissed.

His mind reeled. It was inconceivable to a man who'd lost count of his sexual partners well before he was out of his teens. Yet the small, still reasoning part of his brain acknowledged Lily kissed like a virgin.

Shock ground through his belly. Tangled threads of desire and guilt twisted into a jumbled knot that grew and grew till it pressed upon his chest, cramping his lungs, stopping his breath.

He reared back, panting, heart hurling itself against his ribs. He looked down at parted lips, plump and pink. Almost, he slammed his mouth back onto hers as the tide of wanting rose.

But he forced himself to think. To observe.

Her breathing was even more out of kilter than his, her eyes closed. On one side of her face was clear, flushed skin, soft as silk. On the other, the broad, taut brand of healed flesh. She'd called it ugly, something from a horror movie. To Raffa it had merely become part of her, like the way she wrinkled her nose when he said something she disagreed with. Or the glow in her eyes when she forgot to be cautious and revealed her natural ebullience.

Could it be true no man had got this close because of her scar?

Or maybe she'd been too defensive to let one near. That, he could believe.

Her eyes snapped open, searching with an intensity that made Raffa feel every one of his thirty-three tarnished years.

He could barely remember being a virgin. He'd never kissed one in his life.

As for taking one to bed, as he'd aimed to take Lily after a champagne supper—he shuddered, seeing the awed hope in her gaze. The innocence, for once unguarded.

She trusted him.

Raffa thought of the things he'd done to get where he was today, the seedy, *special* arrangements. He was sullied in ways Lily would never know. Ways that didn't show on the outside, but were there, a stain nothing could remove.

Aghast, he dropped his hands as a new thought needled.

Had he, at some unconscious level, understood Lily's innocence? Was he grasping for it as once, years ago, a jaded businesswoman had lusted after Raffa's innocence as much as his young body and fair face?

Bile rose in a gush. Acid filled his mouth, obliterating the taste of her, the beckoning, elusive flavour of innocent pleasure.

What had he ever known of innocent pleasure?

'Raffaele?' Her whisper tugged his libido and his conscience—two entities that had lain dormant for so long he'd thought he'd lost both. 'What is it?'

Caution clouded her desire. It happened so fast it confirmed everything he'd wondered about the hurt she'd endured in the past. She'd schooled herself to disappointment.

'You're right,' he croaked. 'Dining together is a bad idea.' He cleared his throat, forcing out the words. 'It's better if you leave.'

She spun away before he stopped talking, was out of the villa within seconds. But not before he saw hurt in her eyes. And the way her head rocked back as if he'd hit her.

Raffa stood where she'd left him, sucker-punched by an unseen blow to his belly at the pain he'd inflicted.

Worse, though, was the knowledge he couldn't fix this. He couldn't be the man Lily needed.

CHAPTER TEN

HOURS LATER, LILY still cringed when she thought of the frantic way she'd clung to Raffaele, begging for more.

One touch of his lips was all it had taken for every defence to collapse, laid waste by his caresses and her desperate hunger.

She'd been so needy she'd thought she'd explode with wanting. Another kiss like that and she'd probably have climaxed where she stood. It almost made the years of waiting worth it, to experience such incandescent pleasure.

Raffaele was a master of the sensual arts. No wonder he hadn't wanted to continue the experiment. She'd been gauchely overeager, lost to everything but the wonder of her first kiss.

Twenty-eight and kissed for the first time!

And the last, if tonight was any indicator.

Lily groaned and swung around to pace the darkened room. There was no danger of tripping over anything. She'd retraced her steps thousands of times in the last few hours, unable to settle while she was so awash with fury, frustration and embarrassment.

Why, oh, why had she let him dare her into taking a risk? Into believing after all these years things had changed and her scar didn't matter?

Had she *really* thought Raffaele was attracted to her? The kiss was all about curiosity on his part and she'd left herself wide open to hurt.

Her ribs seemed to contract around her frantically beating heart. She'd believed Raffaele different. Caring, despite his ruthless streak and patent expectation of always getting his own way. She'd never believed him cruel.

But what he'd done tonight…

Oh, get over it! You were only too eager to kiss the man. You can't blame him for pulling back. Just because you're besotted—

Lily slammed an iron bar across that thought. She was *not* going there. Not now. Not ever.

She was going to do what she always did. Pick herself up, dust herself off and get on with life. Bury herself in work. Strive to achieve.

Except she'd left her laptop in his villa and nothing, not even a tsunami, was going to propel her back there.

Her gaze went to the view beyond the window, the pale crescent of sand and dark glitter of water. There was one way she could expel this restless energy. Spinning on her heel, she crossed the room, reeling off her top and bra. Her skirt slithered to the floor and she stepped out of it, then her underwear, tugging pins from her hair. Naked, she grabbed the new swimsuit, obliterating any thought of the man who'd given it to her as she dragged it on. Of course he hadn't chosen it personally.

Moments later she was closing the door of her villa, breathing the sweet scent of blossom in the resort gardens and the tantalising saltiness of the sea. She took a step, only to slam to a halt as she saw something on her private patio.

Someone, not something.

In the starlight he looked impossibly tall as he vacated the chair and stood.

'How long have you been here?' The words were staccato beats, crashing through the silence. Adrenaline blasted her bloodstream, triggering heightened awareness. She registered the residual warmth of the flagstones beneath her bare feet, the throb of her pulse, the prickle as her flesh tightened, responding to Raffaele's nearness. And the lingering taste of him on her tongue, like a delicacy her memory refused to discard.

In the gloom she made out his characteristic shrug. 'A while. I thought you were asleep.'

Lily hadn't bothered with lights. She didn't want to face herself in the mirror. Darkness had been a refuge.

'I don't want you here.' The words scraped from the bottom of her bruised soul.

'I know.' His voice sounded curiously hollow.

'Then why are you here?' She jammed her hands on her hips, finding comfort in indignation.

'I wanted to make sure you were okay.'

'By sitting here in the dark?' She'd never heard anything so unlikely.

'I didn't want to leave you all alone. I felt…responsible.'

Ridiculous how that stung.

'I'm an adult, Raffaele.' She swallowed his name, hating that even now she loved the taste of it. Lily wanted to rage and curse at the power he had over her. It wasn't supposed to be this way. She was supposed to loathe him.

'There's no need to feel responsible. I look after myself.' For a moment she felt the weight of that drag at her shoulders. The years of being alone, dealing with everything solo. Then she straightened. 'Don't wait up for me. I'm going for a swim.'

One swift step and he blocked her path. 'At night?'

Lily angled her jaw, as if she could meet his eyes in the shadows.

'You're not my keeper. Now step aside. There's no need for this…' she waved her hand dismissively '…show of solicitude. Go away and concentrate on Robert Bradshaw. He's the reason you're here.'

She needed to remember that. Raffaele's focus was business. He was single-minded to the point of obsession with this project. She was a curiosity, a diversion.

'You can't swim now. It's too dangerous.' The words sounded as if they'd been ground out, like glass splintering beneath a twisting boot. 'What if you get a cramp and there's no one to help?'

A writhing, seething, lava-hot surge of anger shot through her, that he pretended to care. She sidestepped and stalked past.

Hard fingers shackled her wrist, pulling her up short.

'Let. Me. Go. Now.'

'Lily, listen to me, I—'

'No.' She swung around, staring up into features now illuminated by starlight, features as flagrantly gorgeous as ever. Lily felt the inevitable lift inside her chest, then the slow burn of shame that she couldn't, even now, eradicate the wanting.

'*You* listen, Raffaele. I may be different to the people you know. I may *look* different. But I deserve respect. I'm not some amusing freak, here to entertain you in your downtime. I—'

'*Per la Madonna!*' The low roar of his voice filled the air, his hand gripping hers. 'Don't talk like that.'

'Why not? It's the truth.'

A rush of words filled her ears, low, fluid, a non-stop litany of what had to be curses, though she couldn't understand the Italian. She'd never heard Raffaele sound so far from the savvy, self-contained entrepreneur she knew.

'You can't think that! It's not true.'

Abruptly weariness gathered her in. What was the point of listening to Raffaele excuse his behaviour?

'I'm not interested, Raffaele. Just go. Leave me be.'

'Lily. I swear it wasn't like that.'

'What was it like, then?' She knew she shouldn't ask. His answer would only rub salt in the wound but she couldn't stop herself.

'It was…unbelievable. Better than I'd ever—'

'No! Don't you *dare*!' Lily reefed her fingers from his, clapping her hands over her ears. 'Don't lie.' She spun away, stumbling down the sandy path towards the beach.

This time it wasn't his hand that stopped her. It was his whole arm, looping around her waist, hauling her back against his tall frame. Heat and muscle burned her back. But it was nothing to the fire roaring within.

'It's no lie.' His breath feathered her neck, stirring her hair. 'Kissing you was the best thing I've done in years.'

Lily shook her head. How was she supposed to stay strong when he used words like that to undo her? Despite her indignation, her knees wobbled. She was in danger of sagging against him.

Deliberately she snorted her disgust. 'Right. That's why you pulled away as if you'd been burned. Why you told me to leave.'

'I told you to leave because I realised you deserved better…than I can give you.'

Her bitter laugh tore the night. 'Better? You have to be kidding.' He kissed like a god. What could be better? 'You just didn't like the way I kissed you back. It reminded you that it was ugly Lily Nolan in your arms.'

Sibilants hissed against her ear as another burst of Italian washed around her, rougher this time. His arm at her waist turned hard as iron.

'Didn't like it? You have no idea.' Gone were the smooth cadences of his seductive voice. Instead it sounded like gravel dipped in burning tar. 'If I didn't like it would I react like this?'

He hauled her back so she was plastered against him. Hard thighs pressed into her and an enormous erection rose between the cheeks of her buttocks.

Lily swallowed convulsively, eyes popping, not just at the impossibility of his arousal, but the sheer size.

In this moment, with only the flimsy fabric of her swimsuit and his clothing between them, she felt her inexperience like a brand. The sensation of him jutting against her created a hollow ache between her legs. Even the liquid heat pooling there couldn't fill the void.

'Does it feel like I don't want you?' He ground against her. The slide of his arousal against her almost bare skin was unlike anything she'd ever known, the rough caress of his voice the most potently seductive sound she'd heard. 'Well, *cara*? Does it? You've been driving me crazy.' This time his lips touched her ear as he spoke, sending shivers of pleasure through her.

'I don't understand.'

'Don't you? You might be a virgin but you're not that innocent, Lily. You can *feel* how I want you.'

The shivers turned to a mighty trembling that racked her from head to toe. She wanted him so badly her skin felt too tight, as if she was going to burst out of it. Need and excitement warred with a lifetime's caution.

She was beyond denying her lack of experience. What was the point? It must be obvious.

'But you pushed me away.' Did he hear the hurt she tried to disguise?

'Of course I pushed you away. It wasn't right. You deserve someone better.'

Yet his arm clamped her to him. His body seared everywhere they touched, branding her. And that hard, swollen ridge against her backside... It took everything she had not to arch back, pressing into him.

'That's the second time you've said that,' she gasped. 'It still doesn't make sense.'

The sound of rough breathing filled her ears. His. Hers. The tumult of her pulse. Finally he spoke. 'You're an innocent. You deserve someone who can treasure that, turn your first time into something special.'

'You can't?' It didn't occur to Lily to play coy. Not with need battering her and Raffaele's breath, his body, his words, an enticement she'd given up trying to resist.

His laugh was short and sharp, off-key. He slid his arm across her stomach as if about to release her and Lily grabbed at it, holding on with both hands. His arm was sinewy, dusted with silky hair, every bit as gorgeous as it looked by daylight.

'I have no experience of innocence, Lily. I'm not the man for you.' There was finality in his words. They struck with the resonance of metal on stone.

'I don't believe you.' Releasing her hold on his arm, she twisted round, breasts to his ribs. He was so hot. So heavy against her belly. The weight of his erection made it hard to think. But she wanted him enough to ignore pride and self-preservation.

She slipped her hand, palm down, between them, curving it round his shaft. To her amazement it jumped in her hand as if it had a mind of its own. Her fingers flexed and tightened and she was rewarded with the sound of Raffaele's hiss of shock.

'Don't, Lily.' Hard fingers dug into her shoulders. 'You need someone special for your first time. That shouldn't be me. It shouldn't be anyone *like* me.'

Hands on her shoulders, he stepped back, creating distance. She felt his loss with a keening desperation.

'Don't go. I want—'

'I want too, but it's better this way. You'll find someone—'

'Don't talk rubbish. There won't be anyone else. There hasn't been and there won't ever be.' Not with her face.

For a long, aching moment she waited for his response but there was none.

Defeated, she pulled away so he had to release his hold or follow her. Of course he let her go.

Exhaustion consumed her. The nervous energy that had kept her wired for hours bled away. She'd never felt so weary.

'Just go, Raffaele. I've had enough. I can't follow your logic. You say you want me but you refuse to take me. You say my looks don't matter, but they do. You and I know they do.' Deliberately she lifted her face so what light there was spilled across her features. 'If they didn't you wouldn't hold back. You wouldn't pretend I could choose to make love with you then tell me I can't.'

Lily heard the defeat in her voice and knew she'd reached breaking point. Swiftly she turned, grabbing the door of her bungalow. 'I've never had that choice with any man and I never will.'

Just once, Lily wanted passion, even if only for a night. She wanted to feel as close as a woman could to a man, to experience physical pleasure at a man's hands. Not out of pity or kindness, but because he desired her as much as she did him.

As if that will ever happen.

Worse still, she wanted that with Raffaele. The man she feared she'd fallen for.

Her shoulders jumped as she bit back a silent sob.

The villa door opened easily and she felt sand under her feet as she stepped onto the cool tiles. But the door wouldn't shut behind her. She looked over her shoulder to find Raffaele blocking it, following her inside.

Desperation rose. 'Please go.' She couldn't stomach more conversation. 'I want to be alone.'

He pulled the door from her hand, closing it behind him with a quiet snick, trapping them in darkness.

'I can't '

'Shh. It's okay.' Broad hands reached for her shoulders, drawing her to him, filling her with his spicy scent and that terrible, raw yearning.

'It's not okay.' Her voice hit a discordant note and he heard her fight back tears. 'Please, Raffaele. Please leave.'

Her pain tore Raffa's heart. He'd never heard Lily beg. He hated the sound of vulnerability—worse, of defeat. She was stronger than anyone he knew. He wrapped a hand around her back, the other plundering the silken softness of her hair as he held her close.

He breathed in the subtle sweet-as-fruit fragrance of her skin. He couldn't leave her like this, believing her looks had driven him away. It would only reinforce those negative feelings about her scar.

Raffa told himself he was here for Lily's sake. But he was selfish. He'd followed her because he couldn't walk away, despite knowing he wasn't the man she needed.

'I'm not going anywhere. You're stuck with me.'

'But you said…' Her voice was muffled, her lips caressing his collarbone, shooting sensation to his groin.

'What I said was right. I should go. But I can't. I want you too much.'

Later he'd regret this. Lily would too. But it was beyond him to turn back.

He'd never pretended to be a man of honour. Hadn't he spent his life pandering to excess and self-indulgence? Hadn't he built his fortune on the desire for pleasure? Sure, it had been about providing pleasure for others, but he wasn't spotless. He'd learned to grab what he wanted whenever and wherever temptation offered.

He wanted now.

How badly he wanted.

Bending at the knees, he slipped an arm beneath her legs, another around her back, and hiked her up in his arms. She was all sinuous, lissom curves and smooth, fragrant flesh. Her hair spilled over his bare arm and even that notched his need higher.

Her gasp was loud but it barely registered over the racing thud of his heartbeat as he headed for the bedroom. She'd left her shutters wide open and there was enough light to make out the bed.

His leg hit the mattress and he let himself fall, still cradling her, toppling together but twisting so she didn't take his full weight. Even so, the sensation of her half beneath him sent fire scudding through his body.

'You don't need to do this.' Her voice was half shock

and half bravado. Even in the gloom he made out the tight line of her jaw.

Something, a sensation he wasn't familiar with and couldn't identify, curled in on itself, burrowing through his chest. More than approval, more than pride or even protectiveness.

'You're wrong. I need to do exactly this. I tried not to take advantage, I really did. But I'm not cut out for self-denial.' Not surprising when he'd never tried denying himself anything he wanted, not since he'd worked and finagled his way out of poverty, setting his sights on a better life.

'But—'

Raffa stopped her words with his mouth, damming her protest. An instant later she was returning his kiss with a fervour that shattered his last attempt to hold back. The blaze of wanting consumed them, making her writhe beneath him. His thoughts sped to stripping her out of her swimsuit and impaling himself in her welcoming body as soon as possible.

She's a virgin.

Doesn't that mean anything to you?

The thought diverted his thoughts even as he dragged her shoulder strap down one arm, past the elbow she accommodatingly lifted, and off.

A second later her breast was in his hand, perfect, delectable. He lowered his head, licked a peaked nipple and felt her jerk high off the bed. Raffa stretched out his leg to capture both of hers before he lowered his head again to that stiff peak. He'd thought her taste addictive when he'd kissed her mouth, but this…this made him desperate.

'Please.' Her voice was a moan, her hands clutching him as he drew on her nipple, feeling her shift and buck beneath him.

His erection throbbed against her hip. Much more of this and he'd come before he even got naked.

Lily might be a virgin but she was all passionate woman, and a woman already on the brink.

Pride whispered that it was his seductive skills making her so desperate for release. Logic decreed long-term celibacy played its part.

Twenty-eight and virginal. The thought slowed his urgent touch. For him this surge of desire was remarkable, unique, after years of no interest in sex. But for Lily tonight had to be more. He had to make it perfect.

A man as tainted as he shouldn't be the one to introduce her to sex. But he'd do his damnedest to make it special for her.

Which meant tonight would be all about her.

He looped his fingers under her other shoulder strap and again she helped, eager to peel away the clingy fabric so both breasts were bare.

Her sigh of delight spurred him on as he held her in both hands, weighing those delectable breasts, sucking first one then the other, drawing pleasure from her till he thought he'd go mad from the effort of restraint.

The enticing scent of feminine arousal fogged his brain as he peeled her swimsuit down, over her arching ribs and soft belly, past the jut of her hip bones. His hand brushed the silk between her legs and she shuddered. So ready.

Yet Raffa took his time, rolling the fabric down her legs and away before acquainting himself with the arch of her instep, the slim circle of her ankle, the lush smoothness of her calf. When he kissed her knee and moved higher she sighed.

He followed the sound higher to the smooth flesh of her inner thigh, first one leg, then the other. They were trembling around him as he pushed them wider, jamming his shoulders against her as he opened her to him.

'Please,' she whispered in a purr of sound he knew would haunt his dreams from now on. 'I need you.'

His erection throbbed against the constriction of his

clothes. He wanted to rip his trousers away and thrust his way to release.

Which was why he made no move to undress. He didn't trust himself.

Inching higher, he felt her tension rise. There was something he wanted almost as much as to lose himself in her beautiful body. That was to taste the first orgasm she'd ever accepted from a man.

Lily whimpered as he kissed her there, her fingers tunnelling through his hair, her body restless. He'd barely settled at her centre, had merely taken one slow lick when he felt the fine tremor in her body turn to a judder of building ecstasy.

She cried his name in a hoarse gasp as she accepted the pleasure he gave her, returning it tenfold. Her deep quivers of delight, the tang of her in his mouth and the feel of her flexing, strong yet helpless, beneath him were gifts more precious than he expected. And the way she tugged him close, hands and legs pulling him in, enfolding him as if she couldn't bear to let go...

Had he felt this way before?

The answer was a resounding no.

With Lily he wasn't the cynical man of thirty-three who'd long ago lost interest in women, with their avarice and selfishness. Nor the kid who'd had his first taste of sex as a boy toy of a much older woman seeking diversion. He was someone new.

For years Raffa had used and been used. A commodity craved by women and advertisers who weren't interested in *him*. Never once had he felt as real, as honest, as with Lily.

He lay, centred on her, surrounded by her broken gasps, her trembling limbs and clutching hands, and discovered, to his amazement, it really did feel better to give than to receive. He *wanted* to please her.

Of course he wanted her for himself, but equally he

wanted to bask in her rapture as she learned delight in its many forms.

He lifted his hand, gently caressing her damp curls, and felt her jerk beneath his touch, still so sensitive.

How could he resist an invitation like that?

His expertise with women, his intimate, encyclopaedic knowledge of their bodies, wasn't something to be proud of. He'd acquired it as a necessary skill then later used it to get his own sexual satisfaction quickly. But tonight, as he turned that knowledge to seducing Lily, he was grateful for it. Every touch, every kiss, each slide of his body against hers, each murmured encouragement, had the sole purpose of making her first foray into sex memorable.

Gratification filled him with every sigh she uttered, every sob of delight, every climax. Till finally she lay, utterly spent.

His groin was on fire, his erection impossibly swollen, yet he pulled back.

Tonight was for her.

He couldn't quite believe it, but found himself moving to the side of the bed. Time to let her sleep.

'Don't go.'

'You're awake?' She lay so lax he'd assumed she was out for the count.

'How could I sleep?'

'Close your eyes. You'll sleep soon.' Raffa brushed her hair from her hot brow, feeling an unfamiliar wave of tenderness.

Surprisingly strong fingers caught his wrist. In the darkness he caught the glitter of her stare.

'We're not finished. I want *you*, Raffaele. I don't want to be a virgin anymore.'

Raffa couldn't remember denying himself anything he wanted and he wanted Lily with every fibre. But a decent man would leave her for the lover who, some day, would give her not just sex, but the relationship she deserved. A man nothing like himself.

Fingers shackled his other wrist as he made to move. He could break her hold, but her next words stopped him.

'I'm not a charity case, Raffaele. Don't make me feel like one.' There was just enough light for him to make out the movement of her throat as she swallowed. 'I thought you…wanted me too.'

Did she have any idea how close to the edge her words dragged him? Clearly not.

'Or was all this some elaborate attempt not to hurt my feelings?' Pride was in her stretched-thin voice, but pain too, and defiance.

'You've got a lot to learn about men, *tesoro*, if you think I don't want you.' He yanked her hand from his wrist and jammed it against his chest, where his heart galloped.

He caught the way her eyes widened, then she smiled, slow and wide, with the age-old power of a born seductress.

'Then show me.'

Her hands slipped to his trousers, one fumbling at the button and the other tugging the zip, till he had to rear back lest he lose himself there and then.

A moment later he stood beside the bed, drinking in the sight of her spreadeagled there, her hair a fathomless pool spilling out from her shoulders, her limbs pearly.

A man could only resist so much. He wrenched open the drawer of the bedside table, finding the packet of condoms thoughtfully provided for guests. After that everything blurred till he was naked and rolling on protection.

Then he was on her, flesh to flesh, bone and muscle against sweet femininity, and he was shaking as if he'd never done this before. As if it was his first time, not hers, and he was terrified of getting it wrong.

'This could be a little uncomfortable.' His guttural whisper was unrecognisable as he propped himself above her, taking his weight, holding steady at her entrance.

'You mean it could hurt.' Yet she laughed, as if she felt none of the strain weighing his every movement. 'It's okay. I won't break.'

Her hand slipped down, reaching for him, and instinctively he moved, knowing he couldn't last if she touched him now. The glide became a thrust which turned into a surge of power, taking him deep into close, slick space that opened around him, welcoming him.

There was no gasp of pain, no horror, just a moment of resistance then heaven.

Raffa's breath stalled. He tried to breathe, to calm the pulse storming in his blood, the sharp, rising pull of pleasure. Except Lily confounded him. She wrapped her arms about him, lifted her legs and clung on.

'Yes.' The hot sibilant branded his ear as she rubbed her cheek against his. 'Like that. Please.'

That was all it took for Raffaele Petri, renowned for his sexual expertise and stamina, versed in every carnal art and long past the age of impulsiveness, to buck hard against her, shattering with a roar of anguished delight till the world disappeared in a dizzying swirl.

CHAPTER ELEVEN

HE WASN'T SURE what woke him but for once in his life Raffa wasn't eager to get up. He lay, eyes closed, content to enjoy the comfort of lying here, replete.

Usually he was up straight away, diving into each day with a determination to meet every challenge and win. Today felt different. *He* felt different.

He stretched and immediately stilled, registering warm flesh beneath his arm, against his body. Feminine curves, fragrant and enticing.

Lily.

His eyes snapped open and he found himself staring into a serious, questioning gaze of glowing amber, flecked with brown.

Shock buffeted him.

He'd spent the night in Lily Nolan's bed.

He never spent the night with any woman. They got ideas about permanency and relationships, as if they'd shared more than sex.

Memories bombarded, vivid, intoxicating memories of Lily falling apart again and again. And of him, utterly out of control. Him expecting familiar sexual satisfaction and finding something beyond his wildest imaginings.

Raffa sucked in a breath and slid his hand back from the indent of her waist. It was only then he realised he'd clamped one thigh over hers in his sleep, caging her to him.

As if even in sleep he couldn't let her go.

The mighty erection prodding her belly reinforced that.

'You weren't expecting to see me, then.' Her voice was curiously flat, as if she'd ironed out all emotion. But he felt the sudden rigidity in her, saw the brightness dim in her eyes and the hint of a smile die on her lips.

So it started. The games women played. The emotional blackmail they employed.

Deliberately Raffa stilled in the act of drawing his leg away.

'I didn't expect to see anyone. I sleep alone.' There was a hard edge to his words. He resented explaining himself.

'Then you should have left last night. This is my bed. I didn't invite you here, if you remember.'

'I remember.' She'd infuriated him, worried him, turned what should have been simple sex into something complicated. He'd felt like some dastardly villain when he'd sent her away and she'd fled, drawing the scraps of her dignity behind her. Later, when she'd talked of being ugly and not desirable—he'd been torn between hunger and the fear he'd hurt her even more by taking what they both wanted.

She'd made him confront the dark truth at the core of himself, the sense of being tainted, too soiled to touch an innocent.

Yet he had. He'd given her a night of unabated delight. In the process he'd crossed so many boundaries he'd ventured into unfamiliar territory. A difficult, unpleasant place where feelings burgeoned in the pit of his belly. He felt edgy, like the first time he'd left the warren of familiar childhood streets, not knowing what threatened around the next corner.

Now she looked at him like something she'd tracked in on the bottom of her shoe.

'It's time you left. It's getting late.'

Raffa didn't like the memories her words evoked. It had been years, a lifetime ago, since a woman had shown him the door when his services were no longer required.

He felt a burst of that ancient resentment, as if he were a youth again, frustrated anger at himself for letting himself be used, even if it was his only way out of the hole

he'd grown up in. Shame that he managed to find physical
pleasure when honour dictated he should take none when
money changed hands.

Raffa shoved the memories away. It was a place he didn't
visit.

'Why?' he drawled, his voice harsh. 'You're ashamed to
be seen letting me out of your villa so early in the morning?'

Her eyes widened. 'More like saving your reputation.
I'm sure you'd rather not let it be known where you'd spent
the night.'

On the words she lifted her hand and pushed her hair off
her face, turning her head a fraction so the sunlight spilling
across the bed slanted over her scarred cheek.

Instantly, as if a giant fist smashed into his solar plexus,
Raffa's indignation disintegrated.

Even after last night, after he showed her again and
again how beautiful she was, how much he craved her,
Lily didn't believe it.

'You think your face will repel me?' His voice was a low
growl. As if she'd let a tiger into her bedroom. His eyes
glittered so fiercely Lily felt almost anxious.

There was nothing to be anxious about. She'd had the
sort of night she'd never believed she'd experience, discov-
ering intimacy with the only man who could tempt her to
let down her guard. She'd loved every minute and would
carry the memories for the rest of her days.

Now it was over. Last night's kindness was over. That
was obvious the moment he opened his eyes and reeled
back.

It was time to move on.

It wasn't as if she'd expected he'd want a *relationship*
with her.

'I think it's a new day and it's time we ended this...' Lily
didn't have a word to describe last night. Especially as they

still lay naked together, his thigh imprisoning her hip and his shaft pressed against her stomach. She kept her hands tucked together in front of her, knuckles touching his chest when he breathed deep, locked together so she couldn't be tempted to reach out.

Yet inside her muscles clenched and released and clenched again, feeling the empty ache she'd never experienced before Raffaele had taught her to want him. She wanted him to fill that void, hold her close and take her to heaven. Being with him, sharing that ultimate intimacy had been mind-blowing.

'You say that because you're scared.'

'Scared?' She looked into narrowed eyes and felt herself fall into those blue depths. 'Of what?'

'That last night was real.'

He stopped the protest rising in her mouth when he lifted one palm to her face, flattening it over the taut, uneven flesh of her scar. Slowly he dragged his hand down, investigating from temple to chin in excruciating detail.

Lily's pulse jittered and danced within a body frozen in shock.

'Don't. There's no need.'

He shook his head and this time she thought she read a softening in that bright gaze.

'There's every need, Lily.' He leaned forward so his breath feathered her lips. As if on cue, her eyelids lowered in anticipation of his kiss. Even angry and hurt, she couldn't help responding.

What she hadn't expected was for him to kiss not her lips but her cheek. Her maimed, ugly cheek.

She reared back, pushing him away, but he was already there, lips skimming her temple, pressing her ravaged face. Not feather-light touches either. These were real, deliberate. She felt each caress as if branded. Everywhere from her cheekbone to her jaw, the corner of her mouth and out towards her ear. There wasn't a centimetre Raffaele didn't touch.

Lily's breath clogged. She couldn't twist away; his powerful body and hands held her still.

Pain built behind her ribs, rising in her throat to scratch the back of her mouth.

Finally, finally he lifted his head and the air rushed from her in an audible whoosh, collapsing lungs on fire till she drew in another breath, this one redolent of spice and musk and Raffaele.

It was too much. More than Lily could take. Moisture pricked the back of her eyes, her throat constricting.

On a surge of desperate energy she shoved him with both hands. She must have taken him by surprise because he fell back long enough for her to tug away, half-sitting, dragging her hair out from between them. She grabbed the sheet and—

'Stop running away.'

Lily stilled, closing her eyes as she sought something like calm.

'I'm not running. I just don't appreciate you pretending…'

'Pretending what? To be attracted to you? To not be fazed by the fact you've got a mark on your face?'

A mark! As if it were a mole or a smudge instead of a stonking great—

'Yes!' The word hissed from her as she rounded to face him. Gilded by the morning light, rumpled and angry and utterly gorgeous—the sight of him cleaved a shard of pain through her middle. 'I don't want you pretending anymore. Even though I appreciate what you did last night. Don't think I don't.'

She'd expected something hurried and perfunctory. Instead she'd been gifted with a night that dazzled her senses and made her poor heart ache even harder for something she couldn't have.

'You're a slow learner, Lily. How many times do I have to prove I don't give a damn for your scar?' He paused, his scrutiny so intense she felt it track over her. Then he shook his head. 'You're hiding behind that, aren't you? You're using that as an excuse.'

'I don't know what you're talking about.' Desperate, she swung away, shifting closer to the edge of the bed.

'It's easier to pretend it's your scar holding you back, than that you're holding yourself back from living. Because you're a coward.'

Lily froze. Even her heart seemed to stall.

What did this man want from her?

How many times did she have to prove herself?

She'd left her refuge and crossed the globe at his insistence. She'd worn the clothes he'd ordered. She'd swam for the first time in years. She'd sat out in public, baring her face and body to all those curious eyes. From the first there'd been something about him that dared her to live up to his expectations. As if he knew she was stronger than even she realised.

And now she'd given him her virginity—begged him to take it, abandoning herself utterly.

'You're pushing me away because you don't want to admit you want more from me.'

Lily squeezed her eyes shut, letting her head sink towards her chest.

How did he know? Was she so transparent?

'Why do you say that?' That croak of a voice wasn't her own.

'Because I feel the same.'

Stunned, Lily spun round. Raffaele's eyes were serious, his mouth grim. As if she got to *him* as he did her!

'I don't understand.'

His bark of laughter scratched like clawing fingernails up her spine. 'Neither do I. But I know this. I'm not ready to walk away from you, and I don't believe you're ready to do that either. This…attraction between us isn't any-where near over.'

Lily frowned, hope and horror vying for supremacy. 'You don't sound thrilled about it.'

'It wasn't what I planned.'

Slowly she nodded. She understood having a plan and sticking with it. Goals, achievements, more goals. It was how she lived her life. Nice and orderly.

Until Raffaele had woken her in the middle of the night with that heartbreaker of a voice. Ever since, she'd been living out of her comfort zone.

And enjoying it, she realised. He'd dragged her, kicking and screaming, out of her refuge and into…life, with its risks and fears and triumphs. He hadn't treated her gently. He'd challenged and instinctively she'd responded.

A firm hand covered her fist where she still held her hair, caught in a long twist.

'Maybe it's time to let go a little. Do something un-planned and see where it leads.'

Was he talking to himself or her?

'I dare you,' he murmured.

'What? To have an affair?' She sounded so prim. So uptight. So unlike the woman who'd melted to his touch.

Raffaele leaned closer, his wide shoulders hemming her in. 'I don't care what you call it but I want more of it. Of you. Unless you're frightened.'

Of course she was frightened. Who knew what would happen if she gave in to her weakness for this man, not just for a night but longer?

A shimmy of heat flared in her stomach. Excitement. Desire. Greed.

And something else in the region of her heart. It couldn't really be love. Not after such a short time. Not for a man so patently not for her in the long-term.

But in the short-term…

'I'm not scared.' At least her voice didn't shake.

A smile lurked in the grooves at the corners of his mouth. 'Prove it. Now.'

Abruptly he released her and rolled onto his back, spreadeagled across the rumpled sheets. With languid grace he lifted his arms to rest his head on his hands.

He was unashamedly virile. Her gaze traced the dip and bulge of muscle and bone, the jut of his erection, the glint of golden hair and the flash of sapphire as he cast her a sideways glance.

'Put your hair up out of the way.'

Lily hated being ordered to do anything. Yet Raffaele's throaty growl was the most delicious thing she'd ever heard. And it told her what she felt was shared. Heat catapulted through her.

One-handed, she groped across the bedside table, finding a couple of hairpins. Seconds later her hair was pinned up haphazardly.

'And a condom. On the table.' The growl grew deeper.

She turned, saw an unopened foil packet in the litter and felt that throb of need again. Her hand was unsteady as she tore it open.

Who'd have thought twenty-four hours ago that she'd be doing this? Shocked laughter trembled on her lips, only to die as she turned back and saw Raffaele watching. He looked relaxed as a cat, sprawled in the sun, yet the atmosphere was taut with expectation.

She opened her mouth to say she'd never put on a condom before, then realised it was superfluous. Raffaele knew and was challenging her to deal with it.

Biting her cheek, she shuffled across the bed, bashful despite the sizzle in her blood. Kneeling over him, she concentrated on her task, diverted by the feel of him, silk over steel. Inevitably she fumbled, hearing his intake of breath.

'Did I hurt you?' An upwards glance caught his jaw clenched and nostrils flared as if in pain.

'Absolutely not. Just—' he paused to swallow '—finish what you're doing.'

This time, as she smoothed the sheath down, she watched his face and realised it was arousal creating that stark look on his face and turning the thighs beneath her to granite.

She, Lily Nolan, was seducing Raffaele Petri, luring him to the brink of control. He wanted her here, wanted her touch, even if it was a little clumsy. Wanted *her*.

Warmth spread through her body, like sunlight coursing through darkness.

Lily rose on her knees and shuffled forward. Still he didn't move, though the muscles in his arms and shoulders flexed. She hesitated, wishing he'd help her, give a suggestion, but of course there was none. This was about her taking charge. The notion was decadently tempting.

Lily held him, bracing one hand on the bed. A familiar hot spice scent filled her nostrils. His scent, she realised, not some bottled fragrance. It lured, beckoned, as if she wasn't already in his thrall.

Slowly she lowered herself till they touched. She caught fire in Raffaele's bluer than blue eyes and the quick throb of a pulse in his throat. Then, watching him watch her, she eased down, eyes widening at the slow, inexorable, amazing sense of him filling her.

It was like last night only different. Exquisite closeness, a fullness that seemed greater than the physical act of sex. It filled her heart, making her blink from an excess of emotion.

Lily felt the sun on her scarred cheek, saw her lover's gaze drink her in and the look in his eyes made her feel triumphant, special, even beautiful.

If she could bottle this moment she would. But already it was over, the breathless stillness giving way to restlessness as she moved against him, her eyelids flickering as flames licked inside her. Raffaele's hands went to her hips, steadying her when she quivered and hesitated, yet letting her set her own rhythm.

In the morning light she was fascinated to read the signs of his arousal. The clench of a muscle in his jaw, the way his chest heaved high, his stifled gasp when she changed her angle and his hips rose, driving them harder together.

Delight beckoned, but so did the idea of pleasing Raffaele, returning at least a little of the bliss he'd given her last night.

Planting hands on his shoulders, she leaned forward. His gaze riveted on the swing of her breasts, the gleam in his eyes as powerfully arousing as the sensation of their bodies sliding together in perfect harmony.

Lily grabbed one of his hands and planted it on her breast. Instantly his fingers moulded, kneading, not gently but enough to send pleasure rocketing through her. Her movements quickened, more staccato than smooth, but it didn't matter because Raffaele's thrusts kept pace, faster, stronger, more abrupt.

Again that fierce triumph filled her. This was something she could do for him. Lily snagged Raffaele's other hand, pressed it against her breast, holding his hands in place with both of hers.

His mouth sagged as he fought for air, the tendons in his neck standing proud. That big, strong body was trembling, on the brink, and it was more exciting than anything that had gone before.

Lily leaned down, holding his gaze. When she was so close she felt his breath hot on her lips she whispered, 'I want to watch you come, Raffaele.'

There was an instant of silence. His heavy-lidded eyes blinked wide then she felt it, the out-of-control buck of his body, the rushed surge inside her turning into a pulsating thrust that ignited the embers of her own climax. There was a muted growl that turned into a rolling roar. His hands kneaded her breasts, sending bolts of rapture from her nipples to her womb where the fire burst its bounds, devouring her as it devoured him.

Together they jerked and shook and shuddered and through it all she was lost in his azure gaze, reading awe that matched her own.

It was only as she collapsed, muscles failing in the wake of such a potent climax, that Raffaele shifted his grip, pulling her head down to his. He bestowed a kiss that tasted different to any they'd shared. It was slow and tender and, as she gave herself up to it, Lily realised the last of her defences had shattered.

CHAPTER TWELVE

RAFFA LOOKED ACROSS the wide veranda of the plantation house to the man he was here to meet.

The man he was here to ruin.

Triumph stirred. Soon Gabriella would be avenged.

Yet he found it difficult to relish the moment when he was distracted by guilt.

He'd made a mistake bringing Lily with him, despite her desire to see the place. He shouldn't have subjected her to Bradshaw. The man's first startled look at her face had morphed into distaste before he belatedly put on a smarmy smile of welcome and became excruciatingly over-solicitous.

It had made Raffa want to throttle him. But beside him Lily had merely stiffened, her face turning mask-like. Raffa knew her well enough now to realise that mask hid hurt but she wouldn't thank him for interfering.

'It's a lovely old house,' she murmured. 'I particularly like the full-length windows and shutters.'

Bradshaw smiled expansively and launched into a monologue about the property.

Its bones were beautiful but it had been let go. Paint peeled on the shutters and even from here Raffa could see blank spaces inside where furniture and paintings had been emptied from the sitting room.

If it had been *his* family home Raffa would have cherished it, not left it to crumble and fade.

The thought caught him up short.

What a joke. Raffa had inherited nothing except his face. And the family trait. Everyone in his old neighbourhood knew the Petri women were saints, suffering long and stoically. For the Petri men were renowned sinners, handsome rogues who enticed beautiful women into motherhood and occasionally matrimony, then abandoned them. Sordid—that was what they were.

No wonder he'd ended up as he had.

'Sorry?' He caught Bradshaw leaning forward in his seat, obviously repeating something.

'Mr Bradshaw was offering you a tour of the house.' Lily's voice had a husky edge that reminded him what they'd been doing just an hour ago.

Bradshaw was unable to hide his eagerness. 'Or perhaps we should go inside and get straight down to business. Leave the ladies to themselves.' His toothy grin widened as a woman wafted through the French doors onto the veranda as if on cue.

Raffa noted her studied pose, her sinuous walk, and felt recognition stir. Blonde, tanned and overdressed, she flashed a diamond bracelet and a come-hither smile.

Olga Antakova. One-time model and would-be trophy mistress.

'Raffa. It's been ages.' Her voice purred but her eyes were ice chips. No doubt she was remembering the way he'd bundled her out of his limo the night he'd found her there in nothing but a fur coat and aspirations to live as a pampered sex toy.

'Olga.' He inclined his head. 'This is Lily Nolan.' His voice was warm as he said Lily's name and the blonde's eyes widened.

'How do you do, Ms Antakova. Or should I call you Olga?' Lily shot him an impatient look as if wondering why he wasn't already off, closing the deal with Bradshaw.

Lily could be almost as single-minded as him. Raffa admired that. He enjoyed the way her mind worked, the unexpected depths she brought to any discussion. Almost as much as the way she all but purred her pleasure when he touched her.

He rose, telling himself it was stupid to delay here, feeling protective. He knew Lily could look after herself.

Deliberately he put down his glass and turned to the man he'd been pursuing for so long. It was time to put his offer on the table. 'Lead on, Bradshaw.'

Olga was speaking, reminiscing about an opulent society event where she'd played a starring role. Lily tuned out, realising all she had to do was murmur occasional encouragement.

She'd been nervous on the way across the island, wondering if she'd hold her own with Robert Bradshaw and his guests. Even knowing she looked her best in her new dress, she'd been daunted. Despite her growing confidence, she still didn't like meeting strangers and the thought of a crowd filled her with nerves. But she'd been determined not to hide away as she'd once have done. Besides, there were only two people here, and Raffaele was with her.

Should she be worried that made her so happy?

This…relationship was short-term, she knew that. Yet being with him, feeling valued as an equal and especially as a woman, gave her a new perspective and a new confidence.

Thanks to Raffaele for daring her to confront her fears. With him she was a woman capable of anything. Even bringing the sexiest, most powerful man she'd ever met to trembling desperation.

So what if Bradshaw averted his eyes from her face? As for Olga, she'd dismiss any woman who wasn't as glamorous as herself.

What concerned Lily was Raffaele. Behind the confident air she'd read deep-seated tension. Was this deal really so vital? Bizarrely she'd wanted to grab Raffaele's hand and reassure him. As if he weren't perfectly able to deal with a lightweight like Bradshaw.

'So, Raffa is your boss?' Olga didn't wait for her an-

swer but kept talking. Obviously she couldn't conceive of
Lily as his lover.

Lily shifted in her chair, imagining how she must look
to the glamorous Russian, her damaged face in stark contrast to Raffaele's male beauty.

Then the twist of silver around her wrist caught her eye.
Raffaele had presented her with the bangle to go with the
dress she'd bought on impulse. It was simple yet elegant
and she loved it. It felt like a talisman, reminding her how
unexpectedly wonderful her world had become.

It was the first time anyone had bought her jewellery.
The first time she'd felt comfortable adorning herself. It
had felt momentous, a symbol of a bright new start.

But mostly she'd been thrilled by Raffaele's expression
when he gave it to her. Not only approval but—

'You two work closely together?' Olga drained her glass
and leaned back languidly. Yet there was nothing languid
about her eyes. They were like a cat's, watchful, hungry.

'He must trust you to bring you here.' Olga lifted her
hand to play with her tousled curls and the band of diamonds around her wrist sparkled in the sunlight. 'You must
know if he's ready yet to do a deal with dear Robert.'

Was the woman really so naive as to expect her to betray a confidence?

Olga leaned forward, her voice dropping. 'Robert's been
so reasonable. He even offered a forty-five per cent share
of the resort.' She shook her head. 'If Raffa is interested
he'd better move fast. Others are interested too.'

So that was the deal. A partnership.

Raffaele hadn't mentioned that. He didn't have partners.
He delegated day-to-day management of individual enterprises but he was always the final authority.

Could he change to accommodate a partner?

More to the point, why would he? The resort was charming. But what made it so attractive he'd change the habit of
a career and take a partner to get it?

'Well? Is he here to make a deal?' Olga's eagerness was obvious. Maybe she really cared for Bradshaw.

'Raffaele doesn't inform me of his plans.'

'That one keeps everything close to the chest.' Olga's mouth tightened and Lily was consumed with a need to know exactly what had been between Raffaele and the Russian woman. 'But you must have some idea?'

Did that wide-eyed look work with men? 'That's not something I can discuss. One of my conditions of employment is complete confidentiality.'

The other woman leaned back, surveying Lily speculatively.

'That's why you won't talk. You're in love with him, aren't you?'

'Sorry?' Lily gaped, horrified.

The blonde looked knowing. 'You're so protective, like a mother hen guarding her chick.' She laughed, the sound grating. 'As if that one needs your protection.'

Lily plonked her glass down, every muscle and sinew twanging with shock.

In love with Raffaele.

Olga had put into words the fear, the dreadful yearning hope that haunted Lily. She'd told herself it couldn't be true, but in her heart of hearts she hadn't been able to deny it.

'You have an excellent imagination to read that from the fact I won't discuss his business.' Lily was proud of her even tone.

'It's not just that. There's the way your eyes follow him when he's not looking. You eat him up.'

Denial stuck in Lily's throat. *Had* she made her feelings obvious? Sickening fear rose that maybe Raffaele had seen her stare at him like that. Except Olga had specified 'when he's not looking.'

Lily shrugged. 'He's the most attractive man I've ever seen. Why wouldn't I look? But, as for anything else? He's not my type.'

'Let's be frank. He's *every* woman's type. You'd have to be blind not to be attracted. And even if you *were* blind, he knows his way around women. He's had plenty of practice using those skills to get exactly what he wants.'

It was on the tip of Lily's tongue to say Olga wasn't in any position to throw stones, but she snapped her mouth shut. It was no secret Raffaele's life was littered with women.

Lily told herself she was grateful for all that experience. She had no one to compare him with but if she was destined to have just one lover, she'd lucked out with Raffaele. The way he made her feel...

That was when she realised what it was she read in Olga's sharp gaze. Jealousy.

'Raffaele rejected you, did he?'

Lily's words halted Raffa in the doorway.

He'd left Bradshaw ringing his lawyer since Raffa had given tomorrow as the deadline to agree to his terms. He'd cut the meeting short, not wanting to leave Lily with Olga Antakova. Unease had been a low thrum in his belly all through the meeting.

What he hadn't expected was to hear Lily take the Russian head-on.

'Reject *me*?' Olga's tone dripped ice. 'As if I'd give him the chance. I have more taste than to fall for a man like that.'

Raffa's lips twitched. No, Olga hadn't fallen for him, but she had tried to catch him the best way she could. And been furious when he'd spurned her. She represented everything he despised in the high gloss, low sincerity world he inhabited. Sex, affection, even friendship were tools to get what you wanted. Commodities. The woman was a million light years from Lily.

'A man like what? Raffaele is incredibly attractive.'

Call him shallow, but hearing Lily's words felt *good*. They kept him where he was, just out of sight.

Raffa was used to the hyperbole of the media, those 'sexiest man' tags, and to fawning women. Yet hearing Lily admit her attraction in her trademark husky voice had a surprisingly powerful effect. Despite their passionate affair she'd never verbalised it, except when she gasped his name in ecstasy.

'I prefer a man with more class.' Olga was giving her best aristocratic impersonation, as if born to diamonds and caviar.

Raffa took a step forward, ready to make his presence known, but Lily's words stopped him again.

'Class? If Raffaele doesn't have that, I don't know who does. He's savvy and successful but he's decent too. And kind. Not every successful businessman can say that.'

Decent? Kind?

Raffa had been called many things but never, to his knowledge, either of those. Formidable, driven, impatient— that was his current reputation, if you discounted the usual flummery about his looks. And before that? No, neither word fitted the younger him.

'You're attracted by his rough around the edges past?' Olga's voice was frosty. 'I prefer a gentleman.'

'By gentleman I assume you mean someone who never had to work for what he's got?' Lily's voice was even but the precise clip to her words gave her away. 'I'm more impressed by someone who's worked hard for what he has. I find that admirable.'

Her words shouldn't matter. Words had long ago lost any power over him. But Raffa felt his heart bash his rib cage in a double-time rhythm that snared his breath.

He'd never had anyone defend him.

Not since Gabriella.

It made him feel... He couldn't describe the hot turmoil

rising from his belly, clogging his chest and squeezing his throat. Emotion clawed his vitals.

'Oh, Raffa had to work. But not in the way you think.' Olga's tone was snide. 'I met someone who's sure she came across him when he was young, in Italy. You'd be surprised at—'

'Reminiscing, are you, ladies?' He strolled onto the veranda, watching Olga start.

He raised an eyebrow, but she said nothing. She dealt in poison, but wasn't brave enough for a frontal attack. Particularly since she hoped he would pour money in her lover's greedy hands.

He looked at Lily, reading anger in her gleaming eyes and taut frame. Raffa put his hand on her slender shoulder, enjoying the way she instantly eased closer.

'Olga says she knew someone who knew you in Italy.'

'Really?' He held the Russian's eyes. 'What was their name?'

She snapped her gaze away. 'No one important. She wasn't even sure it was you.'

Raffa said nothing. He'd be surprised if her acquaintance would come out publicly with her memories. Nor would it bother him if she did. He'd done what he had to escape poverty.

Yet he tasted bile.

He'd had enough of this place. Dealing with Bradshaw, staying his hand instead of grabbing the man and demanding he admit what he'd done to Gabriella was hard enough. Walking back to find Olga baiting Lily was even worse.

'Ready to go?' His hand tightened on her shoulder and she lifted her gaze to his.

'Absolutely.' She turned to the other woman. 'Goodbye, Olga.'

He slid his hand from Lily's shoulder and threaded his fingers through hers as they stepped onto the path.

She stiffened. 'You want them to know we're not just colleagues?' Lily's whisper was for his ears alone.

'Does it matter? I'm not ashamed of you, Lily. Or of us.' Though the thought surfaced that she'd be ashamed of him if she knew his past.

Lily squeezed his fingers and warmth filled him. She was passionate but outside the bedroom she never touched him.

Because she preferred privacy?

Or because she thought he wanted their liaison kept quiet? As if *she* were some shameful secret.

It was people like himself and Olga and Bradshaw who should be ashamed! Lily ought to be nothing but proud of herself.

Raffa disengaged his hand from Lily's and looped his arm around her shoulder, pulling her hard against his side. Her curves slid against him as they walked and once more that sense of rightness as he held her stifled other thoughts.

A swift turn of her head revealed stunning eyes, brown with an inner glow of amber. A hint of a smile tugged her lips and something in his chest rolled over, as if his heart belly-flopped against his lungs, squeezing the air out.

Raffa stopped, turning to face her.

She lifted her chin, eyebrows rising in question as she planted her hands on his chest.

Deliberately, aware they were in full view of the house, he lowered his head and touched his lips to Lily's. Her mouth opened, inviting him into a realm of sweet pleasure. Instantly any thought of the outside world, of proving a point, disappeared.

Only the knowledge there were better places to kiss her made him eventually pull back. Her eyes shone and her husky laugh urged him on as he clasped her hand and turned towards the resort.

By the time they'd followed the path through the gardens to his bungalow, Lily was breathless and his pulse strummed a quickened beat. Usually he enjoyed the view of the crescent beach and clear waters. Today it didn't register.

Digging for his key card, he tugged her to the door. Palm to wood, he pushed the door open and kept moving.

It was shadowy in the foyer but he read the gleam in Lily's eyes. Her breasts thrust out with each snatched breath.

'So, you find me incredibly attractive, do you?' Raffa strove for light-hearted but his voice emerged rough and urgent.

'You know I do.' Lily stared back. 'That's not news. You've known that for ages.'

Not ages. She'd concealed her feelings well behind her prickly exterior. His *piccola istrice*.

'What are you smiling at?' Her palms flattened on his chest, reigniting that slow-burning fire.

'Me.' He covered her hands with his, his smile fading. 'I can't believe how much I need you.' And not just sexually.

Her words earlier had affected him. Her praise of his character had echoed inside with every step they took back to the villa. Each word swelled inside him, taking up all the available space, clotting his brain, filling him with a pleasure as unfamiliar as it was intoxicating.

Raffa couldn't explain it. Didn't want to. All he wanted was an outlet for this... fullness, this feeling he was about to burst out of his skin. It had to be sexual. There was no other explanation.

One step and he backed her against the wall. Another and he was between her legs, his thigh pressing up. He watched the convulsive movement of her pale throat as she swallowed.

Releasing her hands, he cupped her breasts, revelling in the way they fitted his palms. Seconds later she was groaning, her head lolling against the wall as he rolled her nipples between his fingers.

Raffa bent to scrape his teeth along her bare flesh where

her shoulder curved up to that delectable slender neck. Another groan and she slumped into him, hands on his shoulders for support.

Teeth gritted in a feral smile, Raffa tugged at her dress, lifting it, yanking at her panties till they ripped and fell, leaving him in possession of downy softness. His fingers probed, finding liquid heat as her thighs clamped tight around him.

Urgent now, his need a compulsion he hadn't a hope of taming, he reefed at his trousers, wrenching them open, shoving fabric away till he was unencumbered, fully aroused and sliding against slick, delicate folds.

There. He grabbed her thigh and hooked it over his hip. Just…there and—

'Condom.'

At first Raffa didn't register the wisp of sound. Not till she said it again, a hoarse gasp that made him shudder into stillness just as he began a long, slow thrust into Paradise.

Heat surrounded him. Lush softness. Their laboured breathing. And within him that urgency, unlike anything he'd known, to possess, to claim, to brand Lily as his.

Air sawed from his burning lungs then in again as he managed shallow gasps.

He fought for control. His brain ordered him to withdraw, take the precautions he always did, protect them both. But his body was in full-scale mutiny. It wanted completion, now. Not just completion but to claim Lily rough and hard and completely.

Raffa winced as, finally, he withdrew. The sense of loss was so keen it knifed like a blade through his belly.

Dragging in oxygen, he bent and fumbled for his trousers. His hand met Lily's, already in his pocket.

'Here.' She pressed the packet into his hand.

Her eyes were like gems, he realised. Faceted, gleaming gems, with shards of honey-brown fire.

'Quickly.'

He didn't need encouragement, was already ripping it open with his teeth, extracting the condom and rolling it on.

Lily sighed as he grabbed her hips and plunged inside. Heat met heat and desire coiled tight. He tried to give himself time by focusing on her, watching her eyes flicker half closed and her ripe lips part. She keened his name in that raw, beautiful voice he knew he was the only man ever to hear and that was all it took to drag him over the edge. Raffa thrust hard and shuddered, desperate to capture that pinnacle and take her with him.

Or perhaps she took him, the waves of her climax breaking around him with the force of an ocean surge.

How long they stayed there, sagging against the wall, Raffa didn't know. It seemed hours before he had the strength to carry her to bed, collapsing with her in a tangle of slick, spent bodies.

Never had release been so cataclysmic.

Never once had he come near to forgetting protection.

Lily Nolan affected him as no woman ever had. Raffa realised that for the first time a woman had real power over him. Albeit a power she didn't realise she wielded.

He wanted to spurn the idea, tell himself it was impossible. Yet as sleep claimed him he gathered her close, revelling in the way she clung to him, and smiled.

CHAPTER THIRTEEN

How HAD HE ever thought Lily ordinary? Her eyes glowed and the late-afternoon light turned her sun-kissed hair to bronze. They lay side by side on the sand, spent from sex and swimming. The small beach he'd discovered beyond the resort was deserted and they'd made it theirs.

It was hard to believe just a few hours ago they'd been at Bradshaw's house. This felt a world away from his polluted presence.

'Olga called you Raffa. Were you close?' The sharpness in Lily's question took him by surprise. As did the realisation Lily had never once called him by the diminutive. Yet the way she said his name felt uniquely intimate.

'No. Never.' He covered her hand, hating the idea of Lily believing he'd been with the Russian. 'I met her on a photo shoot. Later she invited herself into my limo and tried to seduce me.'

Lily gaped and he had to repress a smile. 'You're not joking, are you?'

He shook his head.

'I suppose women throw themselves at you all the time.' What was she thinking? Even now sometimes, he found her hard to read.

'It's not always about me. Most of them want the lifestyle. Olga wanted money, not me.'

Lily nodded as she stroked a line from his damp collarbone down his chest. Her lips turned up in a smile that loosened something inside him. 'At least I'm upfront. You know I want your body.'

'Then we're equal,' he growled, drawing his hand over her breast, feeling that tug of satisfaction as her breath caught and her eyes dilated. She looked like a sea nymph, temptation for any man.

Desire stirred. But it didn't diminish that other sensation, the one he'd felt when they came back from Bradshaw's house. That strange fullness, as if just looking at Lily created feelings that crammed him to the brim.

Sex hadn't shifted it. Instead it had settled deep inside him, bone-deep. Raffa frowned, moving his hand down to clasp the curve of her waist.

'What's wrong?' She cupped his jaw, her brow crinkling with concern. Unlike other women, Lily really cared about him. It was distracting, disturbing. And it felt frighteningly good.

No one had cared about him since Gabriella. He found it hard to accept. He and Gabriella had been close as blood could make them. They'd clung to each other after their mother died, fighting the odds to stay together.

'Nothing.'

Wide eyes surveyed him. He could almost hear that analytical brain of hers whirring into gear. 'Was it something Olga said? About the work you used to do?'

If only it were that simple. 'Raffaele?' Lily leaned close and he inhaled the scent of sweet pears, saltwater and warm woman. The combination went to his head, the look in her eyes exacerbating that sensation of fullness, as if a king tide rose within him. 'What work did you do in Italy?'

Raffa hesitated, torn between a lifetime of keeping secrets and the compulsion to trust someone as he hadn't trusted since he was twelve. He'd felt unsettled, not himself, ever since taking Lily to visit Bradshaw.

Finally she dropped her gaze, and her hand. 'It's probably time we went back—'

'I had sex with women for money.'

The words throbbed into echoing silence, broken only by the soft shush of a wave and the squawk of a seabird.

Lily's head jerked up. 'No wonder you're so good at

it.' She stopped, eyes widening as if shocked at her words rather than his. 'You must have made a fortune.'

Lily's response was so unexpected he almost laughed. Except memories of those days were too bitter. 'Hardly a fortune. But enough to feed and clothe me and get me out of the slums.' He had to push out each word. This was something he'd never spoken of.

'I can't imagine real poverty.'

Raffa swallowed what he was going to say, that poverty could make you do terrible things, things you regretted.

'You don't mind?' He couldn't read her thoughts but nor could he see revulsion in her features. Then he realised what he'd asked. Was he seeking Lily's *approval*? His brow knotted.

'It's in the past. I have no right to mind.'

Yet Raffa found himself wanting—what? Absolution? Understanding? It didn't make sense.

'When I was eighteen I met a woman who knew someone that needed a model. The one they'd lined up was ill and they needed a replacement quickly.'

'That's how you started modelling?'

'Yes. Through one of my clients.' He used the word deliberately. Testing Lily's reaction?

Why was her response so important? Raffa lived his life pleasing himself, no one else. Yet he found his hand tight on her waist and his breathing shallow as he waited for her to speak.

'Did it take long to begin modelling full-time?'

'No. They liked my look. I had more work than I could handle.' His mouth twisted. He remembered their excitement at the combination of his looks and streetwise aura. As if growing up in the gutter was a bonus.

'So you were only doing...the other for a short time.'

Was that a blush?

'Long enough. I was almost fifteen when I began.'

'Almost fifteen?' If he'd wanted a reaction he'd got one.

Lily's voice rose, her fingers digging into the muscle of his upper arm as she levered herself up to a sitting position. 'That's...that's appalling!'

Something crumpled in Raffa's chest. He didn't bother moving but sank back onto the sand.

'That's child exploitation. Wasn't there anyone to protect you?'

It took a few seconds to digest that her outrage wasn't directed at him. 'I looked older.'

'It doesn't matter how old you looked. You were a kid.' He saw anger etched in Lily's features. Not because he'd prostituted himself, but because there'd been no one to stop him.

'They were bored and I was there. I spent a lot of time around the marina where the fancy yachts moored.'

Lily shook her head, her damp hair sliding across her shoulders. 'Where was your family?'

Raffa jackknifed up to sit beside her, resting his arms on bent knees. 'I had none.'

'I'm so sorry.' The hand on his arm was gentle and there was true regret in her voice.

He could grow addicted to Lily's empathy.

'It was a long time ago.' Yet the ache when he thought of Gabriella was real. 'Our father left when I was a baby. I have no idea if he's still alive. Our mother died when I was nine.'

'You said "our."'

Raffa fixed his gaze on a yacht out to sea, its sails pristine white against the bright water. He never spoke of this. Yet the compulsion to keep talking was strong. What could it hurt?

'My sister, Gabriella, died when I was twelve. After that I was taken to an orphanage but I kept running away. I spent most of my time on the streets.'

'They didn't treat you well?' She leaned closer, her warmth countering the chill in his bones as she pressed into his side.

'Well enough.'

'But?'

He looked down to find her gaze intent.

Ingrained caution warred with the desire to let go, relinquish the barrier he'd constructed around himself. Already Lily had breached it, making him experience feelings that defied logical description. It would be easy to distance himself as he always did, except he didn't want to.

'But I was looking for the man who killed my sister.' With the words came an easing inside, as if someone had slashed open thick cords binding his chest.

'Killed?' Shock filled her. She wrapped her hand tighter around Raffa's arm and leaned against his shoulder.

A mighty sigh racked him.

'My sister looked after me when our mother died, or tried to. I was a handful.' Lily heard self-reproach. 'She was patient, honest and *good*. I was wild and she was the one who reined me in. She took the place of our mother but I didn't make things easy for her.'

'What happened?'

'Gabriella took after our grandmother, who'd been an actress in France. She was beautiful. Stunning.'

Just like Raffaele. Lily had wondered how he came by his fair colouring. Even for a northern Italian it was surely unique.

'As long as I can remember Gabriella caught men's attention, but she never returned it. She was reserved. She never went out partying. She never even had a boyfriend.

'Men invited her out but she never accepted. Until that night. She'd met a man who invited her to a party on his boat and this time she went.'

'He was someone special?'

Lily felt Raffaele stiffen. 'No, she went because of me. I'd been hanging around with kids she didn't approve of and I'd been acting up, accusing her of being too strict.

We had a row.' He sucked in a deep breath. 'She was only eighteen herself and trying to manage a boy with the devil inside him. That night she'd had enough. One minute she was telling me why I shouldn't hang about with that crowd. The next she said she needed some adult conversation and she'd go to the party after all. She took off her apron, put on her shoes and headed out the door.'

Raffaele stared out to sea and Lily followed his gaze, knowing he didn't see the beautiful vista before them.

'I followed at a distance. I'd never seen her lose her temper like that and I was worried.' His voice hollowed. 'I should have stopped her.'

'What happened?' Lily needed to know but didn't want to hear.

'She went to the marina where the expensive cruisers were moored for the boat show. I saw her board one where there was a party—people and music and laughter. I figured I'd see her in the morning but she never came home.' A shudder ripped through him. 'Next day she was found floating in the sea. The coroner said there was alcohol and a cocktail of drugs in her system, including one used in date rape. She died of an overdose.'

Lily's breath hissed between her teeth. Horror prickled her skin, making each hair on her nape and arms stand to attention.

'It wasn't your fault.' Slowly she sat up, relinquishing her hold and turning to him. Raffaele swung round, his eyes locking on hers with such intensity she felt scorched. Such pain she read there. Such guilt.

'If it hadn't been for me she'd never have gone.' His voice ground low. 'Despite what the police said, she was an innocent. I knew Gabriella. She'd never been with a man, never had a drink with one before that night. He drugged her and she died.'

'You saw the man she met?'

Raffaele nodded. 'I told the police but they didn't believe me. I gave a description but they said there was no such person to be found.' He snorted. 'As if he'd stay. The cruiser had gone, but I kept looking year after year.'

'That's why you hung around the marina.' And had been spotted by those rich women who thought nothing of taking a young boy's innocence. Lily's stomach curdled. No wonder Raffaele didn't talk about his past. 'But you never saw him again.'

'Oh, yes, I did. Earlier this year.' Raffaele's voice was glacial, the set of his jaw aggressive. 'That's when I discovered his name—Robert Bradshaw.'

Lily goggled, struggling to take it in. 'The same Robert Bradshaw…?' But of course it was the same. The pieces fell into place, the reason Raffaele was so driven with this deal. She'd *known* there was something between the two men.

She read determination in Raffaele's harsh expression and a fierceness that stirred uneasiness.

'How can you want to work with him?'

'It's harder than I thought.' He inclined his head. 'I look at him and I want to wrap my fingers around his podgy throat and squeeze.'

Lily froze at the lethal intent in his voice.

'You can't be sure he's the one responsible for your sister's death. It might have been someone else on the boat.' She wasn't trying to defend him, but Raffaele's ferocity frightened her.

His head whipped around, his stare like the sheen of polished sapphires, cold and merciless.

'It was his boat. His party. He was the one lusting after Gabriella, I saw it in his face. Even if he wasn't the one to dope her, he was still responsible for her safety.'

Lily agreed. He'd invited Gabriella and should have looked after her. From what she'd seen of Robert Bradshaw, he didn't look after anyone but himself.

'So how can you work with him?'

Raffaele's lips turned up in a slow smile that looked…

carnivorous. 'It's worth it. As soon as this deal is done he'll
be dead in the water, financially speaking.'

Lily shuddered at his word choice, her mind going to the
image of a young woman, golden-haired like her brother,
lifeless in the sea. An instant later she was on her feet,
arms wrapped around her torso. Despite the balmy air she
felt cold.

'You want revenge.'

'I think of it as justice.' He was at her shoulder, his eyes
fixed on the distance. He looked as handsome as ever but
the lines of that achingly beautiful face were forbidding,
as if the man who'd made sweet love to her just an hour
ago had been evicted by a stranger. Someone who knew
violence and distrust, who'd been used and abused. Who
was completely closed off.

Lily rubbed her hands up her chilled arms.

'How will becoming his partner get justice for your sister? Once you renovate the resort he'll profit from your investment and your experience. How is that punishment?'

Raffaele would turn the place into an ultra-exclusive,
über-profitable retreat for the rich and famous. It was what
he did. That was why Bradshaw was so desperate to bring
Raffaele into the equation, holding off other interested
parties.

Raffa's smile widened in a way that made her glad it
was Bradshaw in his sights, not her.

'That's the beauty of it.' His voice, like velvet over honed
steel, scraped her nerves. 'He's so caught up in anticipat-
ing a huge profit he can't see anything else.'

'What else is there to see?' Lily stepped in front of him,
forcing him to focus on her. His eyes were bright, almost
feverish, and their expression made her uneasy.

'Bradshaw is massively in debt.' Lily nodded. That was
no secret. 'He's going to give me majority ownership of
the whole island in return for money to cover his most
pressing debts.'

'Olga said a forty-five per cent share.'

'That's what Bradshaw offered, not what I'll accept.'

They both knew Bradshaw would take Raffaele's terms. He was desperate.

'He'd lose control of the resort—'

'Not just the resort, the whole island.'

'But in return he can rely on you to upgrade the place and make it profitable in a way he can't.'

'So he thinks.' Raffaele's eyes gleamed.

'You can't do it?' Lily had never heard Raffaele doubt himself and it took her aback.

'Oh, I can do it. But why should I?'

Lily frowned. 'I don't follow. Surely that's the deal— that you invest and upgrade the place?'

'You'd think so, wouldn't you? Whereas, in fact, all I'm promising on paper is the cash to meet his immediate needs. That's already a substantial sum.'

'You're not tied in to upgrading the resort?'

He shook his head. 'No. Bradshaw just assumes I'll make it a priority because of the amount I'm spending to acquire it.'

'But you're in no hurry.'

Lily's breath escaped in a rush. It was on the tip of her tongue to ask what sort of businessman Bradshaw was, but she knew the answer. Her research had revealed a man of puffed-up self-importance who lived the good life but had no clue how to fund it apart from spending the inherited wealth others had accumulated.

'What are you going to do?'

'Once he's signed on the dotted line? Absolutely nothing.'

Lily frowned. 'What about your plans to improve the resort?' She'd heard the enthusiasm in his voice when he spoke of turning it into a truly special place to escape.

'Plans? I have no plans.' Seeing her confusion he went on. 'Oh, I've got ideas on what would make the place work.

It's a shame, really, when there's such potential here, but I've no intention of turning it into a profit-making venture while Bradshaw owns so much as a centimetre of sand here.'

'And you're ensuring he can't interest other investors to do that, by keeping the majority ownership yourself.'

He nodded. 'Not only that. The agreement I've given Bradshaw binds us both to seeking approval from the other before beginning any form of redevelopment.'

'So he's hamstrung. He'll have no saleable assets or income.' He wouldn't be able to sell his minority ownership nor could he start a new money-making venture himself.

She spun round, her gaze going to the headland at the end of the beach, beyond which the resort villas were scattered. What would happen to it? She imagined the buildings crumbling, vegetation taking over with no one to take care of them. For if Raffaele wasn't going to run the place for profit he wouldn't bother taking care of it.

Lily whipped around to face him as a thought lodged in her head. 'What about the staff?'

'What about them?'

'They rely on the resort for their work.'

He shrugged. 'They'll need to find something else.'

Lily looked beyond him to the gorgeous, deserted waters surrounding the island. 'There isn't anything else.'

'Then they'll move.' He frowned and bent to pick up their beach towels. 'There's always work elsewhere.'

'You can't mean that.'

Raffaele's frown became a scowl. 'Of course I mean it. My sole intention in buying this place is to destroy Bradshaw. I intend to see it through. There will be no resort on this island. No enterprise of any kind.'

Something plunged hard in Lily's belly. Her illusions falling and shattering?

She'd believed Raffaele a man she could admire. More, she'd thought herself in love with him. She'd suffered through the story of his murky past and terrible loss but now… Distress churned and she had to fight to stand straight, not bend double, nursing pain.

Lily thrust her hands onto her hips. 'Most of them have lived here for generations. They've brought up their children here. There's even a school.'

Raffaele's shoulders rose and fell. 'A little collateral damage. But don't worry, they'll be helped to relocate. It's no big deal.'

Collateral damage. The unimportant consequence of an action.

Lily knew collateral damage. That was what she'd been the day Tyson Grady had decided to make his ex-girlfriend pay for dumping him. He'd got what he wanted. Rachel never got the chance to go out with anyone else. She'd died as a result of the acid he'd thrown in her face. And Lily— well, Lily had suffered for being in the wrong place at the wrong time.

Bile rose in her throat, threatening to choke her. The sheer arrogance of these males with their feuds and their paybacks sickened her.

'No big deal? This is their *home*!' Her breath snagged in tight lungs. She met Raffaele's gaze and saw no softening, just fierce determination. 'Doesn't that mean anything to you?'

'They can make their home somewhere else. What matters is making sure Bradshaw gets his deserts. Ruining him financially isn't nearly enough. Just be thankful I'm stopping there and not taking the law into my own hands.' There was a flash of something dangerous in those blue eyes. A flash that sent a quiver of fear ricocheting through her.

Lily's hands fell to her sides. The fight went out of her. Bradshaw wasn't the only one to be duped, was he? Suddenly she felt cold, despite the warmth of the sun and the sand.

'I thought I knew you,' she whispered. 'I thought you were...' Her throat closed before she could blurt out any more.

She'd thought he'd risen above his pain and his past to become someone special. She'd thought him kind and caring because he'd helped her face her demons. Instead Raffaele Petri was every bit as hard and conscienceless as she'd first thought. How could she have been so wrong?

'Lily? Where are you going?'

She shoved out an arm to stop him when he stepped towards her. Then she was stumbling over the soft sand, clumsy in her haste to escape.

CHAPTER FOURTEEN

DANNAZIONE! TWELVE HOURS and still Raffa couldn't relax. He strode the path to the hill at the island's centre, needing an outlet for the furious energy that hadn't abated since yesterday and that scene with Lily.

Women!

One minute she was blinking up at him, sympathy in those glistening eyes. The next she was staring at him as if he were a monster.

Raffa's flesh crawled at the memory. He'd grown used to Lily's smiles. She'd even taken his part in the face of Olga's antagonism. He fought his own battles, but her defence had plucked at chords deep within, strumming feelings that still reverberated, refusing to disappear.

Bradshaw was the monster. Who knew how many women he'd abused?

Raffa broke through the trees to the summit. The ocean lay below him, awash with sunrise pinks and oranges. Bradshaw's crumbling mansion was lit in gold. In the other direction the resort lay sleeping.

Except someone else was up. A tiny figure crossed the white sand, wading into the water.

Lily. No one else swam at this hour. That was why he'd come inland.

He stilled, chest heaving. It wasn't exertion that made his heart crash. It was realising he'd come here to avoid her.

Raffa frowned. As a kid on the street he'd learned never to turn his back on the dangerous or the unpleasant.

If there was a problem, better to face it than hope it would magically resolve itself.

And she was a problem. Lily, the woman who'd unleashed worrying new forces, new *feelings*.

All night he'd wrestled with a disturbing desire to do something, say something, to banish her scowl so she'd smile at him like before.

How weak was that?

Was he going to stop his plan for retribution because some locals would be uprooted? They'd be better off on a larger island. Simple economics meant a bigger population attracted better services and job opportunities. He'd ensure they got help to relocate. Once they'd moved they'd probably thank him for the opportunities he'd provided.

This is their home! Lily's words echoed in his head.

She was too emotional. If there were problems with the relocation, he'd fix them. He wasn't like Bradshaw, using then discarding people.

Yet, annoyingly, doubt persisted. Just because he had no concept of home, was it possible he underestimated its importance?

Raffa folded his arms. It was sentimental twaddle.

He'd never had any attachment to 'home.' Even when his mother was alive, he'd rarely seen her as she struggled to support them. He'd been raised in a series of miserable rooms, each more rundown than the last. Home was where his sister was, not in cold concrete.

Yet the churning inside didn't ease.

It was like those early days, looking through windows to glimpse the secure, happy lives of other families, knowing they might as well live on another planet for all the similarity between them and him.

Lily made him feel like an outsider again.

He sucked in a breath, inhaling the scent of dew and foliage and flowers. That hint of sweetness reminded him of Lily's tantalising scent, understated yet seductive.

She'd inveigled her way into his life, not just his bed. The realisation welded his feet to the rocky ground.

Lily mattered.

He'd opened up to her, telling her things he never shared. He'd sweated on her reaction to his past then been relieved when, instead of turning away, she'd offered understanding. For the first time since Gabriella he'd had someone on his side. Someone who saw *him*, not just a face or a body. For that brief space he hadn't been alone. It had felt…good.

Raffa hefted another breath, eyes fixed on the tiny spot that was Lily, swimming in the bay.

He'd done more than open up. *He'd trusted her.* Despite the fact trust didn't come easily.

That was why he'd let her into his life. Why it hurt that she'd spurned him.

He'd waited last night for her to knock on his door, apologise for abandoning him and admit she'd been wrong.

He'd missed her.

Raffa's chest burned, his whole body was drawn tight. But worse was the raw ache right at his centre. An ache that echoed the loss he'd experienced when Gabriella died.

It didn't make sense. He'd only known Lily a few months. He felt protective after all she'd been through. He admired her brain and her sass and her indomitability. And her body. And her laugh.

And the husky way her voice broke when he stroked her supple body. And how she snuggled against him in her sleep. Because she wanted *him*, not his money or his reputation.

She cared. Which meant she'd see sense eventually. She was probably looking for a way to mend their argument right now. Maybe she was nervous about apologising. He knew he could be intimidating.

His pulse kicked at the thought.

In the distance Lily emerged from the water and crossed the beach towards her villa.

Raffa turned and started back down the path, his stride lengthening.

* * *

'Lily?' He pushed the door open and entered. The living room was empty, the shutters open to let in the breeze. Her laptop sat open on the coffee table beside a bag of liquorice. Raffa smiled. He'd watched Lily nibble the stuff when she was working hard, particularly if she was nervous.

Was she nervous about confronting him? Was that why she hadn't come to him?

As he crossed the room Raffa heard the shower. He was drawn by the thought of Lily, naked and glistening, of joining her and ending their argument with hot, satisfying sex.

He forced himself to turn away. This was about more than sex. He didn't know what this was between them, but he was determined to find out. And to find out, they had to talk.

Raffa frowned. Such thoughts were a foreign language, unfamiliar and difficult. Unease prickled between his shoulder blades. Did he really want to go there?

Restless, he stalked to the lounge, grabbing the laptop as he sat. Might as well see what updates Lily had done overnight. There'd be something—a nugget of information on the old plantation estate or some snippet about Bradshaw. The deal would be wrapped up in a few hours when Bradshaw signed. Yet still Lily insisted on working. Unless news of his scheme had changed all that. Suddenly he needed to know.

One tap and the screen came to life. Not a report, but an email.

Raffa was about to minimise the document when the title grabbed his attention.

Re: Island Deal—Urgent.

Maybe it was relevant after all. He scanned the text. It was brief. And it sent shockwaves through him.

Your report was excellent. More needed asap, especially on the counteroffer. What can you dig up? Cash bonus if you get me the info and we seal the deal, plus a week as my guest at the resort.
De Laurentis

Raffa gritted his teeth. De Laurentis. The savvy hotel developer who'd caught him out two years ago on that Greek deal. The one he'd outbid for the Seychelles property.

De Laurentis, asking Lily to provide information on a counteroffer for an island resort.

Raffa stared, the text on the screen blurring. There was a roaring in his ears, like the charge of a hundred motorcycles revving in his head. His belly contracted into a seething mass and pain radiated along his jawline as his teeth ground together.

De Laurentis.

And Lily.

Lily feeding De Laurentis information to rob Raffa of the deal with Bradshaw. Robbing him of his revenge.

'Raffaele?'

Lily hoisted the towel higher across her breasts. Her heart careered madly as wild hope rose.

He'd come.

All night she'd tossed and turned, wanting to go to him, wanting things to be as before. But she hadn't because what he planned was just plain wrong. If she went to his villa he'd seduce her with his beautiful body and rich voice and those big, clever hands. With the way he made her feel special.

She swallowed hard.

If she let him seduce her into acquiescence to his scheme she'd feel tainted, as if she'd betrayed the people who lived here. After all, it was her meticulous research that had got him here, poised to take over Bradshaw's business and close the resort.

But he'd come. He was ready to talk.

'Raffaele?' She loved saying his name. She loved—

He swung his head round, those bluer than blue eyes zeroing in and her buoyant lightness faded. It wasn't tenderness or understanding she read in his face. It was something that made her flesh pinch as if an army of venomous ants swarmed over her, nipping and stinging till she felt hot and distressed.

He shoved her laptop aside and stood.

Instantly she was aware of his superior height. Fury radiated from him as clearly as light from a bonfire.

'You've been busy.' His voice was soft. Not soft like a comfortable embrace but lethally soft, lifting the hair on the back of her neck.

'I've been for a swim.' She took a step forward, vowing not to be intimidated by the man she'd come to care for. He was angry because they took different views on his plans but they'd work through that. She'd already decided she needed to speak with him as soon as possible. Emerging to find him already here just made it easier.

'And you found time for work as well. What a busy woman you are.'

Despite her reassuring self-talk, Lily stopped short. She'd heard Raffaele demanding, angry, reassuring, even tender, but never sarcastic.

'You pay me to work.' It was a matter of pride that even though she was having an affair with the CEO, she still did her job.

'And so do others.'

Was that why he looked so grim?

'You know I've got other clients.'

'Not when I pay for your exclusive services.'

Lily's heart stilled then rushed into an uneven rhythm.

The way he said *exclusive services* made her think of something other than her research.

Heat scorched her breasts and throat. She wished she was fully dressed instead of draped in a towel, her wet hair slick down her back.

'The work is all but done. You said so yourself. My staff needed a hand on a project—'

'I pay for your time, end of story. I told you to clear your other work away.'

'I know but—'

'But nothing, Lily.' He stepped around the end of the lounge, stopping square in her personal space.

Normally that wouldn't matter. Normally she'd be reaching for him, eager to run her hands over his shoulders and into that thick hair, tugging his head down to hers.

But the current of energy running between them wasn't like that. This felt dark, troubling. Threatening.

Lily hitched her chin. 'What's the problem, Raffaele? All I've done is answer a few emails and—'

'And what?' It struck her that for the first time in ages there was not a hint of softening in his eyes. They looked hard and cold as rock crystal. 'And sold a report to my rival?'

'Sorry?'

'Don't play coy. I read the email. You're doing business with De Laurentis. You're selling him information, aren't you?'

Lily frowned. What had that project in Thailand to do with Raffaele? As far as she knew, he had no interests in that part of the world.

'I finalised a report for him weeks ago.'

'And now you're sending him inside information.' He leaned close, his breath brushing her lips. 'Have you forgotten the confidentiality clause in your contract? I can sue you for everything you've got and could ever earn if you betray me.'

Lily stared, reading nothing but antagonism and a thirst for blood, her blood, in that big, bold face.

Her throat scraped raw with the force of her indrawn breath.

'You think I've betrayed you?' Understanding dawned. 'You think I used the information you paid me to find and passed it to someone else.'

'Not just someone else. The only serious rival I've got. And not just the information you unearthed.' His voice was like the lash of a whip. 'I've shared things with you—my plans to take Bradshaw down. The fact I'm not going to give him what he wants—a profitable business he can leech off for the rest of his days. I *trusted* you.'

'You honestly think I betrayed that trust?' Lily's head jerked back as if he'd slapped her. 'You think I shared what you told me in confidence?'

She should be furious. Yet somehow all she felt was pain. Pain that he'd think so little of her. That shimmering joy she'd found with him had been an illusion, as insubstantial as a pool of water on a bed of sand.

'What else can I think? You're dealing information to my biggest rival. Or do you deny it's the same De Laurentis who made a name for himself with top class hotels in Italy? The one now investing in coastal resorts?'

'It's the same man, but—'

'But nothing!' As if hearing the way his voice had risen, he paused. When he spoke again his voice was slow, deliberate and barely above a whisper. 'I pay you an exorbitant salary. I expect discretion and loyalty.'

'I have been discreet and loyal.' The same discretion and loyalty she gave all her clients. Which was why she hadn't told Raffaele when she began working for him that she'd already committed to this job. De Laurentis deserved the same consideration Raffaele did. 'There's been no sharing of information.'

'You expect me to believe that? The man says he's desperate for information you can *dig up* on a counter-offer for this resort.' Raffaele didn't move yet seemed to swell, growing taller, more menacing. 'Well? Speak up.'

This was the man she'd fallen in love with.

The man she'd entrusted with her fragile hopes and dreams. The man she'd leaned on as she forced herself from hiding and into the world.

Hot tears spiked behind her eyes. Distress grabbed her throat and she had to work to find her voice. She laced her fingers together, squeezing.

'Despite how it looks, he's talking about another property. On another continent. I didn't tell you because I didn't see a conflict of interest at the time. They're completely separate. But, because of what's happened between you and me, I was about to write and tell him I can't work for him anymore.'

Lily had known that no matter what happened in the future, whether she worked for Raffaele or not, she couldn't work for his competitors.

'You expect me to believe that?'

Lily stared into that stony face, each beautiful line carved as if in granite. Into eyes that sliced through her. She'd swear she felt the cut right to the bone.

She'd turned herself inside out for Raffaele. He'd burst into her life and made her face her deepest fears head-on. He'd seduced her into believing the world could be an entrancing place, that *she* could be someone she'd never dreamed she could be.

He'd made her love him. And, worse, believe he might care for her, just a little.

And now, in one fell swoop, he'd smashed it all. The hopes, the joy, the trust.

That grim face held no doubt or tenderness. She'd made a monumental fool of herself. What had she been—a diversion? A curiosity? Reclusive and virginal and so naive. Someone a little different for a holiday fling.

Pain raked at her insides.

It wouldn't have hurt as much if he'd accused her of being unattractive. But he'd attacked her in the one place she'd always relied on. The one part of her life where she'd been strong and confident and sure of herself. Her professionalism. She'd believed in that when she'd believed in nothing else. And now he tried to smash that too.

'No, I don't expect you to believe it. I can see you've made up your mind, no matter what I say.' She hauled in oxygen and planted her hands on her hips. Somewhere, deep within, dreams were disintegrating, hopes vanishing. But one lesson Lily had learned well —to conceal hurt.

'There's nothing more to say, Raffaele. In the circumstances, I know you won't want me to work out my notice before I resign.'

Silence. Blankness on his features.

What had she expected? Second thoughts? An apology?

'You can resign tomorrow, *after* I close this deal. And know that if you try to pass any more information to De Laurentis in the meantime, my lawyers will make it their mission to destroy you.'

Silently Lily nodded. Words were beyond her. It took all her energy just to stand tall, bearing the weight of each lashing word.

He turned, glanced at the laptop, and she wondered if he was going to smash that too, or take it with him. Instead he strode to the door without looking back, confident in the knowledge no sane person would ignore his threat of legal action.

Clearly he expected simply to walk out of her life, dismissing all they'd shared. As if that, and she, meant nothing.

'You told me about your past.' Her voice was croaky but she knew he heard. 'The way you spoke made it sound like you felt…' She paused, searching for the right word. 'That you felt *diminished* because of what you'd done to get out of poverty.'

Raffaele stopped, his hand on the door. He didn't turn.

'It's not what you did for a living that taints you. It's the fact you haven't learned to trust anyone but yourself. Until you do you'll always be alone.'

She snatched a heavy breath.

'You made me trust you, Raffaele.' Lily almost choked on his name, but fought back despair. 'I hate that you've shattered that trust. But I intend to be stronger than you. I'm not going to let that destroy me. I'm going to get on with my life and not look back.'

For a heartbeat he stood unmoving, then without a word he dragged open the door and strode into the sunlight.

Had she really expected him to listen?

Lily stood in the centre of the room, rigid with shock. A forlorn, disbelieving part of her hoping he'd return when he calmed down.

He didn't return.

She stood so long, not daring to move lest the hurt inside break free and smash her into tiny pieces. But eventually her legs gave way and she staggered to the lounge.

Fifty minutes later she was on the motor launch heading for the next island. Two hours after that she was airborne, beginning the long trip away from Raffaele.

CHAPTER FIFTEEN

AT LAST IT was done. Bradshaw had signed the papers and Raffa was the majority owner of the island.

He should be crowing with delight, or at least smiling with satisfaction. Instead he felt a sense of anticlimax. As if this long-awaited victory wasn't everything he'd hoped for.

There'd been a moment of predictable, if shallow, pleasure when he'd refused Bradshaw's offer of a champagne toast to celebrate their partnership.

There'd been several minutes of gratification as he'd explained precisely why they would never work together. And the fact that he, Raffa, intended to ensure the island would never make a profit to support the man responsible for killing Gabriella.

Bradshaw had blustered and denied and finally pleaded, but the legal documents were watertight. He didn't have a leg to stand on.

Raffa had listened to Bradshaw ranting and threatening, and waited for the welcome surge of pleasure.

It didn't come. Instead he felt unsettled. Something gnawed at his gut. He and Consuela were almost back to the resort when he realised it was because justice, or vengeance, or whatever you named it, couldn't bring Gabriella back. The hole in his heart was still there, still raw. He'd failed her. If he'd been a better brother—

'My legs aren't as long as yours. Do you mind slowing a little?'

He glanced at Consuela, impeccable as ever in a severe charcoal suit. Interestingly, she didn't look like she'd just achieved a major victory either.

'Sorry. I was thinking.'

'Not happy thoughts. I assumed you'd be pleased.'

He shrugged and gestured for her to precede him where the path through the trees narrowed.

'I've got a few things on my mind.' Not just the unexpected sense of let-down but that scene this morning with Lily. His thoughts had circled back to her words time and again, even when signing the all-important contract.

'Something to do with Lily?'

Raffa's eyes fixed on the woman in front of him but she didn't look back, just kept walking.

'Why should it be to do with her?'

'Because when I arrived at the airport I saw her crossing the tarmac to board a plane.'

Raffa stumbled on the perfectly even surface of the path. 'Lily?' He'd only left her a short time ago. 'You're mistaken.'

Consuela stopped and turned. Her expression was neutral but there was something in her eyes he didn't recognise. 'I know Lily, remember? It was definitely her but she didn't see me. She looked…'

'What? How did she look?' Tension hummed through him, drawing him tight.

Consuela's mouth tightened. 'Let's just say that if the security staff hadn't stopped me I'd have gone over and given her a hug.' Her eyes narrowed and now he recognised her expression. Disapproval. Of him.

'But our flight isn't till tomorrow.' Why he said it he didn't know, except he was struggling to grasp the fact Lily had gone. He felt like someone had blasted a gaping hollow in his chest. He braced his feet wider.

It didn't make sense. He should be pleased to be rid of the woman who'd betrayed him. She'd saved him the necessity of travelling with a corporate spy.

Except ever since he'd accused her he'd felt *wrong*.

As if he were the one at fault.

As if he'd missed something.

As if he should have taken time to listen to her protests of innocence.

Doubt had beaten at him from the moment he'd left her but he hadn't let himself weaken and return. He'd had too much on his mind—his plan to exact justice on Bradshaw.

Now he felt as if he'd got his priorities wrong.

'Tell me. Who else was sniffing around this deal? Who else courted Bradshaw?'

Consuela's eyes widened but she rattled off names. Big leisure company consortiums. The ones he knew about.

'Anyone else? De Laurentis?'

'No, but Lily is the researcher. You should ask her.' One perfectly arched eyebrow rose. 'The last whisper I heard was that he had his sights on something in Asia. Thailand, I think.'

Raffa closed his eyes, a sick feeling dragging at his belly. He'd jumped so eagerly at the idea Lily had betrayed him. Had he *wanted* to believe it? Was it easier to believe the worst than try to live with the unsettling feelings she stirred? What did that say about him?

'Raffa! Are you okay? You look like you're going to keel over.'

He snapped his eyes open, finding no comfort in Consuela's concern.

'Speak to me. What's wrong?'

He lifted his face to the sunlight filtering through the trees. Way above was the wide blue arch of sky where Lily was flying away from him.

Realisation skewered him like an insect on a pin. It was an effort to draw breath and his voice, when he found it, was choked. 'I've just made the biggest mistake of my life.'

'So you'd call yourself a digital nomad, Ms Nolan? Working all around the globe? How do you find that?'

Lily smiled at the woman in the dark suit at the front of the audience. 'Lily, please.' She gripped the podium, not with horrible nerves as when she'd started her presentation, but because it was comfortable.

After visiting her family, joining the women's business breakfast group was the first thing she'd done on her return. She hadn't wanted to. She'd wanted to bury herself at home and stay there. Which was all the proof she needed that she *had* to do this.

She'd been shaking with nerves before each meeting, especially today, but came away each time feeling better than before. This was the first time she'd presented and initially it had been tough. Standing in front of all these people, sharing insights into her enterprise, was the test she'd set herself. Proof that she could and would be strong.

Which was a laugh, given how forlorn she felt. Only the determination to keep busy stopped her from curling up and weeping into her pillow. She wouldn't go back to the woman she'd been before Raffaele had forced her to change.

'Like anything, there are positives and negatives. I can work almost anywhere—'

'Just give me the chance to work on a tropical island,' someone said and there was a ripple of good-natured chuckles.

'It had a lot going for it.' Lily's smile grew fixed as an image of Raffaele filled her brain. The touch of his hands, the velvet tone of his voice, the bliss they'd shared, the sheer, dizzying delight.

And the abyss of pain.

She blinked and refocused.

'But it's still work, wherever I'm located, so access to a reliable network is vital. I couldn't risk long power outages, for instance, so I'd give storm season in the tropics a miss.' She forced a smile into her voice.

'And there are benefits to being in an office, face to face with colleagues. I'm currently looking into ways to make that happen regularly, so my team and I aren't always working in virtual isolation.'

'I'm afraid that's all we have time for this morning.' The MC made her way up to the podium, smiling.

Lily was returning her smile when a ripple of unease skated across her flesh, tugging her body to alert.

A whisper coursed through the room. Lily saw heads turn, not towards her as the MC thanked her and the audience applauded, but towards the back of the room.

Lily shook hands, said something suitable and widened her tight smile. But she didn't hear what the MC said about upcoming events. It was drowned by the thump of her pulse as slowly, with a feeling of inevitability, she lifted her gaze towards the rear exit.

Raffaele. Large as life and more gorgeous than she remembered.

Her knees loosened to wobbling jelly, making her grab the podium for support. A mere couple of months wasn't nearly long enough to get over him.

She'd known it was Raffaele from that first prickle of awareness, that familiar soaring sensation inside. Yet she hadn't believed it.

Fate, and Raffaele, couldn't be that cruel.

But it seemed they could.

The MC struggled to get the crowd's attention. But every woman had turned to watch Raffaele, suave and appallingly handsome in his trademark open-necked shirt, casual jacket and pale trousers that emphasised the length and strength of his powerful limbs. Lily's heart slammed her ribs in a stop-start beat that left her breathless.

His eyes met hers and she'd swear she heard a whoosh of flame as her body ignited.

Or was that her paper-thin defences? She wasn't ready to face him. She needed more time to look convincingly unaffected. Despair lashed her.

The MC said something, motioning her towards the side aisle of the auditorium.

Gaze still locked on Raffaele, Lily stepped away from

the podium, forcing her head up and shoulders back. She prayed she wouldn't stumble on those cotton-wool legs but refused to watch the ground. This was the man who'd used then discarded her like a piece of trash. She'd meet him eye to eye with no hint of weakness.

Vaguely she was aware of the audience watching, of excited whispers. But it was the whispers filling her head that nearly undid her. *Cara, tesoro*, and all those other Italian endearments he'd used in that deep velvet voice.

Lily told herself he'd used them deliberately to get what he wanted—the novelty of a twenty-eight-year-old virgin in his bed. Because if he'd meant any of them he'd have listened to her explanation, given her a chance. He'd have believed her.

She stopped close, staring into azure eyes that reminded her how he'd taken her to heaven. Ruthlessly she shut the memory down, licking her lips to moisten her parched mouth.

Instantly his gaze dropped to her mouth and her breath stalled. One look! That was all it took for him to turn her inside out all over again.

'I presume you want to talk with me?' Her voice was steely. She was amazed at how firm it sounded.

His eyes jerked up and she was surprised at how distracted he looked. How far from the determined, decisive CEO who'd ruthlessly cut her adrift.

For a moment he looked about to speak. Then he nodded and held open the door. The whispers grew to excited speculation as the door swung closed behind them.

'You've changed.' He hadn't meant to blurt it out but he was shocked.

Not by the way Lily had held the audience in the palm of her hand. He knew she was capable and a good communicator when genuinely interested in something.

Nor was it her new clothes that surprised him. She

looked good in slim-fitting trousers, heels and an amber silk top. More than good. He wanted nothing more than the freedom to run his hands over her body. Explore the satiny skin of her breasts and inner thighs that no silk could match. Let down her hair and tug her into him.

She swung her head round so their eyes met and there it was again, that punch to the gut. That frigid glitter. That total lack of welcome or warmth.

His belly tightened as terror tugged his vitals. It wasn't new. It had grown familiar since she'd gone. Yet he'd hoped for a glimmer of warmth.

'Of course I've changed. You taught me a lot.' Her mouth twisted and he felt searing pain. 'I learn from my mistakes.' Then the shutters came up.

She looked like a duchess surveying a beggar. Despite a lifetime pretending not to care, concealing emotions and revelling in the success and wealth he'd acquired, this time it mattered. It reminded him of his pedigree of poverty, his grubby past and every sordid encounter. Worse, it spoke of the way he'd mistreated her. Her disdain sliced to his soul, carving through the vast emptiness inside.

How had he thought he had a chance?

'Raffaele?' Her eyes rounded and for a fleeting moment her hand brushed his. The silver bangle on her wrist caught his eye and his heart pounded with excitement.

That touch, that moment of concern, and the fact she wore his gift, were all it took for hope to rise. Not because he really stood a chance, but because he had to try. He couldn't go on like this.

'We need to talk.' He quickened his pace, ushering her from the building. His hire car was parked at the kerb but she walked on when he would have opened the car door, her stride biting the pavement.

'Here.' It was a café. Not private. Not what he'd planned. But he'd take what he could get.

He followed her in, past empty tables and a display of

cakes. Lily hesitated before taking the furthest table, tucked
into a corner. Raffa grabbed a seat, wondering if she realised she couldn't get away unless he moved. He doubted
it. She looked distracted, her gaze skittering around the
room.

There was silence till they'd ordered and received their
coffees. Raffa took a sip and moved the cup away.

'Not up to your high standards?' Disapproval laced her
tone.

'I'm not thirsty.' He had no idea how it tasted. His mouth
was full of the metallic tang of fear. He leaned towards her.
'I'm sorry, Lily. So sorry.'

Her cup clattered back into its saucer, coffee spilling
onto her hand.

Raffa heard her hiss of shock as he grabbed her wrist,
pulling it towards him, reaching for a napkin at the same
time to blot the hot liquid.

'Don't! I'm all right. I—'

Her words stopped when he lifted her hand, pressing
his lips to the spot the liquid had seared. Raffa closed his
eyes, a shudder of longing passing through him at the taste
of Lily, as sweet and enticing as he remembered.

Pain battered his chest.

'I'm sorry. I can't apologise enough. I accused you of
something I should have known you'd never do. I wronged
you.' His lips moved against her skin, his eyes shut to block
out the rejection he knew he'd see in her face.

He'd never thought himself a coward but he was now.
He couldn't bear for her to send him away. His grip tightened on her slender wrist, turning her hand so he could
plant a kiss on her palm.

She shivered. From horror? Distaste? Or pleasure?

Raffa forced his eyes open but kept them trained on that
small, pale hand, noticing the tint of amber nail polish as
her fingers curled over her palm.

His beautiful Lily. He'd feared she might withdraw into

her shell again but she was stronger than he gave her credit for. She'd emerged from her cocoon and nothing, not even a lout like him, would drive her back. He was proud of her.

'Why are you smiling?'

'Because you're even more beautiful than I remembered.'

Instantly she tugged her hand. But he was stronger and he'd use any advantage he had, even brute strength.

'Don't.' She sounded choked, not indifferent. 'You've had your fun. Just leave me alone.' Pain pierced at the hurt in her shadowed eyes and the crooked line of her mouth.

'You think I'm here for *amusement*?' Raffa stared. 'There's nothing amusing about my feelings, *tesoro*.'

'Don't talk like that.' Again she tried to free her hand and failed. 'I know it was…diverting to have a woman so different.' Her voice was a rushed whisper. 'But that's in the past. You can't make a fool of me like that again.'

Holding her wrist, he felt her pulse beat a runaway rhythm almost as fast as his own.

'I know you think you can't believe me after the way I rejected you.' He swallowed a knot of guilt and pain at the memory. 'But one thing you must understand. I was never *amused* by you. You were never a *diversion*. You were the most frighteningly real thing to happen to me in as long as I can remember.'

Raffa clasped her hand in both of his. 'No one else has made me feel the way you do.'

To his despair she shook her head, her mouth a mutinous line. 'You didn't feel anything. You turned on me. If you'd really felt anything for me—'

'Oh, I feel, *piccola istrice*. See how much.' He pushed her hand against his chest, spreading her fingers wide over the place where his heart crashed. 'I feel so much I'm terrified you'll turn me away without a hearing. Or that after hearing me out you'll say you're not interested.'

She blinked, an arrested expression in her eyes. 'Not interested in what?'

He shook his head. 'First I need to apologise properly and explain—'

'Not interested in what?'

This wasn't going as planned. He'd worked out what he needed to say, how he'd say it, and she was turning it all on its head. Turning *him* inside out.

'In me.'

Time stretched out like a bungee cord yanked almost to breaking point.

'I've already had you.'

Raffa couldn't prevent the grunt of pain her words dragged out. His chance was slipping away and he couldn't stop it. Panic nudged closer.

'I'm not talking about sex.' The way she shot a glance over his shoulder at the café behind him told him his voice had risen but he didn't care.

'If you're not talking about sex, what then?'

He swallowed, his mouth dry with fear. Had he ever, in his life, laid himself so bare? It went against every instinct of self-preservation to put himself in anyone's power.

'In me. Body and soul. Heart and mind.' He felt her shiver and hurried on before she could stop him. 'I love you, Lily.'

To his horror he saw her eyes well. He reached out and cupped her cheek, brushing dampness from the corner of her eye with his thumb.

'Don't cry, Lily. Please.' It felt as if she'd wrenched his heart out.

'What do you expect me to do when you say something like that?'

He swiped his thumb over her lush lips, feeling them quiver. 'I *want* you to say yes. That you'll stay with me.'

'I can't think when you do that.'

'Good.' His heart soared at the news. For once he did the

decent thing and pulled back. But he stayed close enough to see how the amber at the centre of her irises glowed as if with an inner fire. Always that had been a sign of Lily's pleasure, or excitement. Or emotion.

'How can you love me? You acted like you hated me that morning.'

'And I've regretted it ever since. I couldn't even concentrate on the deal with Bradshaw because I was too busy regretting my behaviour.'

Her forehead crinkled. 'Then why did you? If you loved me—'

Raffa captured her other hand, holding them both tight. 'It won't seem sensible to someone as logical as you, but feeling the way I do——' he swallowed '——loving you, petrified me. I've never loved anyone except my sister and mother. With you I feel *more*. I care about you, Lily. About making you realise how special you are. About your happiness.'

She opened her mouth and he pressed a finger to her warm lips. 'I trusted you with things I've never spoken about to any other person. I felt drawn to you in ways I didn't understand and it terrified me. I think that's part of the reason I reacted so violently to the possibility of you betraying me. It was easier to push you away than put myself on the line and ask you to love me back.' He drew a slow breath, redolent of coffee and sweet pears and warm female flesh.

'I was frightened you'd reject me.'

Reluctantly he dropped his hand from her mouth. He'd run out of words. Which meant facing her judgement. Desperately he tried to read her thoughts, but Raffaele was stuck on her trembling mouth.

'How many women have rejected you, Raffaele?' Her voice was a thick whisper.

Instantly he was defensive. 'Those women in the past don't count. They didn't know or want me. They wanted

my money or my body.' He paused. 'Except I suppose they
do matter. Why would you want a man who—?'

Lily tugged her hand free and pressed her palm to his
mouth. 'Stop right there.'

She smelled so good, like the dreams that had plagued
his sleep since she left. He slicked out his tongue, tasting
her, and her hand jerked back.

'I don't care about the women in your past.' Was it really possible?

'Then what do you care about?' Was that a softening
in her expression?

'Why would you fall in love with me? It's not sensible.'

'I think it's the most sensible thing I've done in my life.
Fall for a woman who's generous, beautiful, sexy, honest,
and challenges me to be a better man. I've even rethought
my plan for the resort because of you.'

To his horror that beautiful mouth wobbled again. 'How
am I supposed to resist you when you're so…?'

'In love?' For the first time since he'd arrived he felt his
heart lift. 'Desperate? Ready to do anything?'

'Honest.' She shook her head. 'If you really do feel…'

'I do. I love you, Lily. I've been falling for you since the
night you seduced me long-distance with that sexy voice.'

Her eyes widened but a smile fluttered at the corners
of her mouth. That smile was like warmth on a freezing
winter night.

'I've been falling for you since we sat on your rooftop
and you listened to me talk about my hopes and dreams.
You were so understanding.'

Raffa stilled, all his senses focused on Lily and the
words she'd just used.

'Falling for me?' Was it possible after what he'd done?

She nodded and a flush crept up her throat. 'I've been
in love with you for ages.' Her whisper all but stopped his
heart. Unfamiliar heat prickled the back of his eyes.

'Raffaele?' She put her hand to his cheek. 'Are you all right?'

He cleared his throat. 'I honestly don't know. I've never felt like this.' At least he knew what this feeling of fullness was, of fear and hope. 'I've never loved anyone like this.'

Her mouth widened into the most beautiful smile he'd ever seen. 'Neither have I.'

For the first time in his life he was lost for words. But not for long. Old shame and new regret hadn't quite died. 'I don't deserve you.'

'Nonsense. You're the best thing that's ever happened to me.' Amber fire sparked in her gaze as if challenging him to disagree. 'By far the best thing.' She paused. 'But I have a question. What is it you call me—*picc...*?'

Raffa grinned. He couldn't help it. He'd never believed such happiness existed. Even the prospect of facing his beloved's wrath when she learned he'd been calling her his little porcupine couldn't dim his smile.

'Why don't we go somewhere more private so I can explain?'

'Why don't we?' Lily placed her hand in his and he knew he was the luckiest man in the world.

EPILOGUE

LILY SMOOTHED HER palms down the scarlet silk skirt of her halter neck dress. Her sexy matching sandals slowed her walk to a sinuous, hip-tilting gait.

The outfit had seemed perfect in the resort boutique but she couldn't help having second thoughts. Maybe something a little less obvious would have been better.

'Lily!' She turned to see Pete from the New York office waving a glass from beyond the pool. 'Great party.'

Beside him Consuela, resplendent in a caftan of blue and purple, chatted with the resort's head butler who, with the rest of the staff, had been given this weekend off.

The island was in carnival, all work done by staff brought in for the duration as everyone involved in redeveloping the resort enjoyed a well-deserved party before the opening next week.

Calypso music filled the air and laughing children wove between the adults before jumping into the pool with the maximum possible splashes. Lily laughed too. Raffaele had done something special here. She was proud of him.

After Robert Bradshaw heard what Raffaele intended for the island it had been easy to persuade him to take cash for the rest of his claim to it. According to Raffaele, that meant after he paid off his debts he'd have enough to support himself on the equivalent of a modest wage for a couple of years. More than enough time for him to find an honest job. Though Lily couldn't imagine him working.

Now the island was a shared enterprise. The resort workers whose families had lived here for generations were the principal owners and Raffaele a minority shareholder. It had been a staggeringly generous gesture but it made ev-

eryone happy, not least Raffaele, who seemed to think he
had to atone for his past.

Lily didn't care about his past, so long as she could help
him make his future all it should be.

She wove through the party towards the new restaurant.
There was Raffaele in conversation with the head chef. Lily
slipped her hand under Raffaele's arm.

Every doubt she'd had about her dress dissolved as he
turned and took her in from head to toe. The gleam in his
eyes told her everything she needed to know but he said it
anyway. 'You look gorgeous.'

His lips were gentle on hers but she felt the way he held
himself in check, because she felt the same. When he lifted
his head his smile was just for her.

'You'll have to excuse me, Henry,' Raffaele said to the
chef. 'There's somewhere else I need to be.'

'Sure.' Henry grinned. 'I'll see you later.'

Raffaele made to pull her closer, but Lily stepped back,
threading their fingers together. 'Not here.'

Eyebrows raised, he followed her, patiently waiting as
they left the celebration behind and finally emerged on the
path behind their private beach. Through the trees stood
the shell of what would be their sometime home. Raffaele
had offered to relocate to Australia but Lily had refused,
for now happy to move wherever business took them.

'What is it, my love?' His voice, that rich-as-caramel
caress, wove its magic and she melted into him.

'There's something I need to know.'

'Hmm?' He dipped his head to nibble her neck and Lily's
head lolled back, warmth filling her. But still nerves prickled her nape.

She'd planned her words carefully, but they were fading from her brain. Raffaele had the power to undo her.

'I want to know if you'll marry me.' The words shot out
before his sensual assault stopped thought.

He stilled. Eyes brighter than the heavens met hers. They

were questioning, stunned. 'You want to make an honest man of me?' The hint of humour couldn't hide his doubts.

'You're already an honest man.' He didn't speak of it but she knew he still felt guilty over his past. Lily threaded her hands through his thick golden hair and pulled his head down. 'You're the only man for me, Raffaele. I want to be with you always.' She watched him swallow hard. 'Unless marriage makes you uncomfortable.'

'No!' He wrapped his arm around her waist, his other hand warm at the back of her neck. 'If you really believe it would work—'

'I *know* it will work.'

'Well, then.' He pressed a tender kiss to her lips. 'We both know I rely on your advice on all important projects.'

'Is that a yes?' Lily's heart skipped.

'You think I'd let you go now?' He shook his head. 'I may have a lot to learn about relationships and feelings but I'm not crazy. Of course it's yes. I want to spend my life with you, *piccola istrice*.'

'I am *not* your little porcupine.' She pushed his shoulders in mock outrage, enjoying how he pulled her close so she felt his muscled body through the thin silk.

'No? But I so enjoy soothing you—' his big hand traced fire down her breast '—till you let down your guard.'

Lily sighed. 'Sounds like a lifetime's project.'

His lazy smile stole her heart all over again. It was brighter than the sunrise and warmed her to the core of her being. 'That's the plan. And I've never looked forward to anything more.'

* * * * *

If you enjoyed this story, check out these other great reads from Annie West:

A VOW TO SECURE HIS LEGACY
SEDUCING HIS ENEMY'S DAUGHTER
THE SHEIKH'S PRINCESS BRIDE
THE SULTAN'S HAREM BRIDE

Available now!

Uncover the wealthy Di Sione family's sensational secrets in brand-new eight-book series
THE BILLIONAIRE'S LEGACY
beginning with
DI SIONE'S INNOCENT CONQUEST
by Carol Marinelli,
also available this month.

MILLS & BOON®

MODERN™

POWER, PASSION AND IRRESISTIBLE TEMPTATION

A sneak peek at next month's titles...

In stores from 14th July 2016:

- **The Di Sione Secret Baby** – Maya Blake
- **The Playboy's Ruthless Pursuit** – Miranda Lee
- **Crowned for the Prince's Heir** – Sharon Kendrick
- **Marrying Her Royal Enemy** – Jennifer Hayward

In stores from 28th July 2016:

- **Carides's Forgotten Wife** – Maisey Yates
- **His Mistress for a Week** – Melanie Milburne
- **In the Sheikh's Service** – Susan Stephens
- **Claiming His Wedding Night** – Louise Fuller

Available at WHSmith, Tesco, Asda, Eason, Amazon and Apple

Just can't wait?
Buy our books online a month before they hit the shops!
visit www.millsandboon.co.uk

These books are also available in eBook format!

0716/01